This book is a work of fiction. The characters, incidents, and dialogue are drawn from the author's imagination and are not to be construed as real. Any resemblance to actual events or person, living or dead, is entirely coincidental.

Excerpts were taken from Robert Frost's poem, "They were welcome to their Belief" published in Scribner Magazine, August 1934.

All scripture quotations were taken from King James Version of Bible.

Revised November, 2016

First Published March, 2015

This book is dedicated to the memory of

Charlie (Papa) and Effie Vannie (Mama) Runnels

And their children

Katherine, Hardy Fred, Myrtis, Myrtle, Jasper Charles, Curtis, Martha, Connie Mae and Patsy.

Chapter 1

Stretching her slender arm to the other side of the bed, she feels the coolness of wrinkled sheets, which tells her that he is no longer in bed. With eyes still closed, she pulls his pillow over to her face, lies against it and enjoys the smell of him.

The smell of his pillow reminds her of pajamas that she has folded away in her bottom dresser drawer. Two sets of men's pajamas, one set, red and grey plaid, and another, navy blue. She had taken the pajamas from the Veterans hospital, over ten years ago, on the day her father died. They are the only material thing she had taken to remember him.

On occasions when she feels the need, she pulls out the now threadbare bundle, the fading scent ever so soft now. She holds it to her face and she is near her father again.

The two men she loved dearest, similar in so many ways. She often wonders, "Do we marry men like our fathers or do we create them?"

As always, he has been up for hours. She hears scudding at the foot of her bed and looks up to see him pulling a brown argyle over his gray turtleneck sweater.

"Where are you off to?" the words barely audible through her sleepy lips.

"I have stuff to do."

"Um, put on a coat, its cold out." She replied, pulling his pillow closer and turning over and returning to sleep.

After a relatively warm winter, the weather had turned rather cold, icy rain had been falling for the last three days. And the streets and sidewalks are covered with an icy slush.

An unrelenting slither of warmth settles on her left eyelid. Drowsily, she recognizes it as sunlight. She struggles to open one eyelid and peers over at the huge silver outlined octagonal clock on the wall.

“11 am, time to get up,” she thinks.

Slowly she peels away the covers and allows her body to adapt to the cooler temperature of the room.

She lets one foot then the other reach the wooly white rug on her side of the bed. She grabs his winter robe, which was lying across the large upholstered chair at the foot of the bed. She rushes to tie the sash against the chill of the cold room.

Through the sun room, into the kitchen, she reaches over to touch the red button, turning on the Keurig for a single cup.

Walking through her office, she presses the on button for her computer, and almost simultaneously twists the wane opening the window blinds.

Returning to the kitchen, she collects her coffee cup, goes back to her office and sits at the computer. She has vowed to discontinue the practice of spending so much time on social media.

“Have to get the morning news and find out how everyone is doing”, she reasons and justifies this action.

Thump, thump, thumpthump thumpthumpthump

“Damn squirrels, damn Elliot” she thinks, watching as one, then another streak of brown jumps from the roof and scurries across the street.

She swears that, on more than one occasion, she has seen the same squirrel stop to look both ways before crossing the street.

She had told Elliot this and he had gotten quite a laugh out of this at her expense, referring to her need for psychotic medication.

He had to admit though, the neighborhood squirrels were an adventurous lot, especially the ones that would jump from the trees in front of an approaching car and sprint in the middle of the street, to see if they could avoid being hit.

Elliot called this game “Squirrel” as opposed to “Chicken”. Only once had he seen a squirrel lose, a fluff of brown fur lying helpless in the back alley.

Just two days ago, she had almost purchased what had to be the perfect solution to the Squirrel- roof problem, if not the perfect solution, then a solution. If she had followed her own mind, she would have….

The doorbell rings; she looks out the window. It’s the cleaners. Leaving her desk, she crosses the living room, her slippers making clicking sounds against the travertine stone tile. In the entryway, she opens the massive and ornate wooden double front doors, which once stood in a grand eighteenth century Spanish chapel. Elliot had brought them back on one of his many business trips to Spain.

Smiling she greets Ernesto, who smiles back at her. Rosita and her husband Ernesto are housecleaners who come once every two weeks to clean the house.

“Happy New Year” he says mid-smile. “Happy New Year to you,” she replies and waves to the figure still seated in the tan SUV outside.

A quick view of the three golden glitter encrusted angels leaning against the wall, two four-foot green artificial wreaths lying in the middle of the floor, and other disassembled Christmas decorations strewn over the living and dining rooms convince them that today was not the best day for cleaning. Next Monday, they agreed, would be much better. This would give her and Elliot time to put away the decoration and get a much more effective cleaning.

Ironic, she thinks. Who would have ever thought that I would someday be able to hire a housecleaning service?

Back at the computer, she remembers a time some 20 years ago. She was a preteen girl looking into the pleading eyes of four of her younger siblings. They had not eaten in over a day and they were hungry as was she. But her concern at that moment was how to feed them.

They stood behind her as she made one more trip to the refrigerator, which at this point contains only a half box of baking soda and an onion: An onion that someone had taken a bite of since the last time she looked into the refrigerator.

She looked at their tearing eyes and wondered how she could get to their grandparents. It was so much simpler before they moved. In Clover Grove, both sets of grandparents had been within walking distance.

“What are we going to do, Jules?” asked the baby girl. This would not be the last time that her baby sister in distress would ask her this question. And again she would not be able to provide a suitable answer.

Jules, whose given name was Julianne, did not reply.

She could think of only one reason that their parents had not been home to provide dinner. They must both be dead. She couldn't bring herself to say that to her siblings. But she wondered to herself.

Never before had they been without food for an entire night and day. While the meals could not qualify as exotic cuisine, they were tasty and filling.

The decision was made; she would have to walk to her grandparents to get food. Julianne took a few minutes to discuss safety with her younger siblings.

"Don't get close to the heaters and don't turn the gas on the stove." Wrapping herself in her warmest coat, socks and boots, she set out for the long walk to her grandparents' homes in Clover Grove.

Before jiggling the door knob to ensure that the door was locked, she yelled one last set of instructions. "Get into bed, pull the covers up and stay there until I get back."

After walking for a half mile she heard the noise of a car behind her. Without looking back she moved to the side of the road. The car pulled up and stopped. She looked over to see her father's weary, yet handsome face. He didn't smile or speak, just stopped the car so that she could get inside. She went to the passenger side, opened the door and got in. They did not talk all the way home.

Arriving at home, she followed her father inside. The smell of fried chicken and boiling rice greets them at the door. Noises of happy children clamoring filled the house.

Nobody asked about the parents' absence. Nobody dared. However, in the months to follow, the father would be an emphysema patient at the Veterans Hospital fifty miles away and their parents would be headed to divorce court.

Chapter 2

For as long as anyone could remember the Sumpners had lived in *Clover Grove.* Approximately 100 wood-shingled roof homes, dotted the clover covered hills of the community.

Alan Sumpners, Julianne's great-great-great grandfather was said to be one of the founders of the community.

Clover Grove had gotten its name because of the thick patches of various shades of green clovers that grew on and around the trees and on to any unattended bit of earth. Because of the clover, most of the grounds in the Grove were in some state of green throughout the year.

Highway 47 which stretched from one end of the county to the next, cut a path almost in the center of the community, and was its main artery. Black tar paved streets, which branched off the highway, were its veins. At the end of each vein were groups of five or more homes where lived generations of families.

This was the community in which Julianne and all her siblings had been born and had grown up. It was the only home she had ever known. It was a community in which she felt safe.

Her paternal grandmother, Louise, lived at one end of the street, a cousin and her husband next door and her maternal grandparents, Ella and Corbin Sumpner, lived on the other end, just before the road curved. She, her siblings and parents had lived in the now vacant three bedroom bungalow between their cousin and maternal grandmother.

There are many legends about the Grove, but perhaps the most frequently shared and passed from generation to generation was of how the *Clover Grove* came to be.

According to legend, there were once identical twin brothers who went hunting for deer. They happened upon the most beautiful young lady that either had ever seen. She was picking flowers near the creek.

Each of the brothers swore himself to one day marry the beautiful maiden. The maiden could not choose between them, since they were equally handsome and brave.

The brothers decided that there was only one solution. They would fight until the death and the one remaining would have earned the right to marry the beautiful maiden.

Tearfully the maiden protested, to no avail; the brothers would not be dissuaded.

And so, weapons chosen and drawn, the battle began. Brian, the younger struck the first blow, followed by an equally powerful blow from Breen, the older.

Soon blood was drawn; at the first sight of blood the brothers knew that their love for each other was too great a bond. Neither could spill the blood of the other.

And so, weapons thrown aside, they began arm-to-arm combat. The two, virtually equal in size and power, wrestled from moon to moon. For days, weeks, months and years, they wrestled non-stop.

Year after year the struggle continued until their bodies became entwined. As the years passed, their bodies began to stretch and transform into vines of silvery green clover. The vines wrapped themselves around and over every tree in the Grove. The battle continues today, as the clover grows inch by inch.

This is a story almost every child who grew up in the Clover Grove has heard many times. Most people believe that there is some truth hidden in this tale, but no historian yet has been able to prove or disprove it.

Chapter 3

Ella and Corbin Sumpner were the parents of nine children. Aileen and David had both died long before Julianne was born.

Aileen, the first born child, was hauntingly beautiful; an oval face, wavy dark auburn hair hanging to her waist, and beautiful almond-shaped, deep hazel eyes. Aileen had been a feeble child prone to colds, flus, whatever illness the weather brought. Yet, she held a special place in her father, Corbin's heart.

It was not because she was sickly or that she was the first born that endeared Aileen to her father. It was her beautiful eyes. Her eyes seemed to have witnessed events centuries old. Eyes that reminded him of someone he had known long ago. Someone he had last seen when he was 10 years old. They were the eyes of his mother.

Aileen was never one to rely on her illness or weakness when it came to doing her share of work around home. At 17 years old, she had become an active teenage girl attending classes during the day and spending her evenings between homework and helping her mother in the kitchen, preparing meals for the family.

She had caught the attention of a local boy, who lived about a mile down the road. Michael and his family, the Crenshaws, were family friends. They attended the same church as the Sumpners. And both families anticipated making wedding plans soon.

One of Aileen's chores was to feed the chicken and collect eggs from the hen house. It was early spring and the evening light lasted a bit longer. There was a slight chill in the air. And so Aileen grabbed her yellow woolen shawl, which was hanging near the door and the basket for eggs and headed out the back door toward the hen house to retrieve eggs for the next morning breakfast.

Thinking to herself, she began to sway, "What a beautiful moonlit night. Next month we graduate high school and then I become Mrs. Michael Alexander Crenshaw….. Mrs. M.A. Crenshaw…... Mrs. Crenshaw…..Aileen Crenshaw." She began to hum as she kicked at small rocks in her path on the dirt-covered backyard.

The hens came in all sizes and arrays of color combinations. She knew each of her mother's prized hens by name. There was Sky, the Ameraucana, named so because of her beautiful dark blue feathers. Mother collected most of her eggs for hatching new chicks. There was Victoria, a yellow and white American Game, named because she was so feisty and protective of her chicks. There was the escape artist, Flight, an Ancona who tended to fly, jump and hop her way over the five foot wire fences surrounding the hen house. Her favorite was the black and white speckled feathered California grey, which she had named Dot.

As she approached the barn door, she heard someone calling to her, whispering, "Aileen, Aileen". Thinking to herself, "If that is Hugh and Carlton trying to scare me with another grass snake, then they will be sorely surprised when I hit them with this egg basket."

Leaving the hen house, she went to the back of the barn and there stood Victor, one of her male classmates. To her, he looked like he had just crawled through a pig's trough and smelled twice as bad. She had seen Victor around school but had never spent any time with him.

Before she could ask him why he was there, he pushed her hard against the barn wall and attempted to press his lips against hers. She pushed him back and raised her leg to kick him. But her leg was caught by another set of hands. She fell to the ground hard, kicking and attempting to scream. Hands belonging to a third person covered her mouth.

Hands were forcing her against the ground, while hands held her legs apart, while hands tore at her clothing. As soon as she would rip one hand from her body, another would take its place. Someone, she couldn't tell who, pushed up her skirt and pulled down her underwear. Tears covered her face as she tried to yell but only managed a muffled whimper.

She was fighting with every ounce of strength that she could muster. She could feel something slimy enter parts of her body that she had never explored. Blunt ended… firm… slimy! She looked into Victor's green eyes and thought surely she was looking at the devil. She tore one hand loose and embedded her nails into Victor's neck. She tried to lift her head so that she could bite into his face, his neck, anything she could reach. But the hands holding her head were too strong.

On Victor's face was the ugliest of expressions. An expression unlike any she had ever seen on another person's face. He was making grunting disgusting sounds, sounds that were unfamiliar to her. Two other faces looked down at her; faces she did not recognize were grinning while holding on to her legs and her arms. They too were making these disgusting sounds.

Unable to move her head, her eyes darted left then right, searching, hoping, praying to see her father.

And she cried….. She cried because there was no one there to help her. She cried because she had done nothing to deserve this vile attack. She cried because Michael would no longer want to marry her. She cried because this was all her fault.

And ….she cried.

"Aileen, are you out here? Aileen!" she recognized her sister Anna's voice. "Aileen!"

The three men released her and fled into the tall woods behind the barn. Victor whispered, "If you tell anyone, I will say that you did this because you wanted to."

Aileen didn't realize how long she had been gone. She had no awareness of time. She wobbled to her feet and pulled on her underwear and straightened her skirt. She couldn't let her little sister, Anna, see her so disheveled. Brushing at her hair, she walked to the front of the hen house.

"Here I am," she said. "I thought I heard a wolf around the back of the hen house and I went to check, but there was nothing."

Anna, in the dark of the evening, could not clearly see Aileen's face. The two girls walked across the dirt covered yard, through the back door and into the kitchen. Aileen went immediately to the bedroom she shared with her two sisters. As soon as Aileen entered the bedroom, Amy, Anna's twin sister, looked at her and gasped.

"What happened to you?" Amy asked.

"Shhhh, I can't tell you." Aileen responded.

"Either you tell me, or I call for Mama right now," argued Amy.

Chapter 4

Looking at the image of the handsome young man in the mirror moving the tassel from one side to the other, Michael thought almost aloud,
" Two more weeks until graduation."

On her way to the kitchen Carol passed her brother's open bedroom door. She couldn't resist the temptation, and smirked,

"Your head is too big for that cap."

Michael ignored her and continued to admire himself in cap and gown. On her trip back from the kitchen, she put her head inside the door, and repeated,

"Your head is way too big for that cap."

This time Michael was prepared and threw his football shaped pillow at her as she ran dodging down the hall to the safety of her own room.

Michael Crenshaw, tall, muscular and yet incredibly thin was a senior at John Logan Bryant High School. A gifted athlete, he played football, soccer, and basketball and ran track.

Michael lived with his parents and sister, Carol. His family had lived in Clover Grove since he was in middle school, when his father's job had transferred the family to the southern part of the state.

Though Michael was a popular student, he was also a very serious one. His parents teased that he had started to plan his life at the age of five. Though humorous, it was not far from true. Michael had always known just what he wanted to do with his life.

He would finish high school and go to work at the mill where his father was production manager. He would work there until he earned enough money to purchase three horses and fifty acres of land. Land that had once belonged to his grandfather. He would build a small house in the center of the land and barns for the horses. He would raise and breed show horses. This had always been his dream. He would travel the globe competing and training show horses.

Friends thought of Michael as an all-in kind of guy. Once he was committed to something, he was there until the end. This made him an ideal leader for the football team, as well as the debate team.

Because he had committed to leading his teammates, leaving his old school and transferring across country to a new school in seventh grade was unusually difficult.

On his first day at the new school, Mrs. McAllister, the seventh grade English teacher had assigned him to seat 14. Walking down the aisle looking for his seat number, he noticed the person in the seat across the aisle from his.

This person was leaning over, trying to retrieve something from under the desk. Beautiful reddish-brown hair almost hung to the floor. He thought to himself. "Wow, somebody's got a lot of hair.

He looked at the number on the desk in front of him, number 14. He was bending to take his seat, when suddenly the desk across the aisle slipped and crashed to the floor. He instinctively reached over to grab the student's arm. This was the first time he saw her face. He was looking into the most beautiful hazel eyes that he had ever seen. They reminded him of the special stones his grandfather, a self-proclaimed amateur archeologist, had brought back from a fossil dig in the Arizona desert. It was like looking into two brilliant circles of amber. And at that moment, he made a modification to his plan. This would be his wife.

For the next four year, Aileen and Michael were inseparable. Both the Sumpner and the Crenshaw families felt that it was an acceptable conclusion that the two would be married after high school.

The next two weeks seemed to crawl by. Michael carried on his regular schedule, reporting to classes every day, lunch with Aileen, then soccer practice, then his part time job at the feed store.

He had noticed though, a change in Aileen. She had become unusually distracted. She was no longer talking about graduation or wedding plans. She seemed lost, far away. Unless someone mentioned their pending marriage, she would not mention it. For months, her main lunch time topic had been commencement and the party to follow.

Must be nerves, he thought. Commencement and Graduation must be making her nervous.

"Tonight will be the best night of my life," he thought, walking over to the bookshelf, picking up a small navy blue velvet bag. He untied the golden cord and pulled out a small black jewelry box. He lifted the lid, to reveal a small gold band with a small diamond in the center. Engaged, he thought. Me….engaged to the most beautiful girl in Clover Grove, in the state, in the world.

"Tonight," he thought "will be the best night of my life. "

"Mike, mom says it's time to get dressed." Carol yelled from somewhere down the hall.

"I'm driving my truck", he yelled back.

"She said it's still time to get dressed."

"Okay, out in 15 minutes." He yelled.

With one leg in his black slacks, he hopped over to the side of his bed, stopping long enough to put in the other leg. He sat on the side of the bed and pulled on his freshly polished black cowboy boots.

Standing, to look at himself in the mirror, he pushed one arm, then the other into a stiffly starched light blue shirt. He grabbed his brush and gave his thick brown hair a quick smoothing before walking out the door.

Chapter 5

"Will you tell him tonight?"

"Aileen, will you tell him tonight?' Anna asked again sitting on the edge of the twin bed.

Aileen sat at the dresser pretending to brush her hair. In the last month her hair had begun to grow faster and thicker than it ever had. Her hair was so thick now that she often had to ask one of the twins to help her brush through the back.

She couldn't understand what was happening until week five passed and she had had no menstrual cycle. When it became increasingly difficult to fasten the buttons on her skirts, she was sure. She was pregnant.

Aileen thought, how can I tell a man who has never done anything more than kissed my lips, who respects me as his future wife, who has vowed not to touch me until we are married, how do I tell this sweet man that I am pregnant with someone else's child?

Finally she spoke, "I can't."

"But how can you marry a man without his knowing that you are pregnant?" Anna asked, rising from her sit on the bed. "You just can't marry him."

Amy, who had been sitting in a spindle back chair at her desk, her back to them, turned to face them. "Anna, what do you think she should do? If she tells Michael she is pregnant, his family will not allow him to marry her.

If she tells Papa what happened, he will probably kill the men and go to prison for the rest of his life. Don't even think about what this will do to Mama.

Then she will be just a pregnant woman living in the Grove with no chance of marriage, an insane mother, and a father in prison. She would be the subject of gossip for all the old biddies in the Grove. We have to agree that we will never discuss this again. We must agree today that we will never tell anyone else. Agreed?"

"But tonight is Commencement Celebration. Michael will probably ask you to marry him soon. What will you say?" Implored Anna

"I'm just saying Michael is such a good man, I don't think he deserves to be fooled."

Aileen did not respond. For weeks she had been lost in a dense fog of endless boundaries. A deep, dark fog was intent on consuming and destroying her very existence. No happy thoughts could break through this fog, no thoughts of graduation, commencement party or even Michael. Aileen sat and continued to brush her long auburn hair.

Finally, Aileen turned away from the antique walnut dresser, "Look girls, I haven't decided what I will do. But right now I need to get dressed for Commencement. Can you two help me do that?" she asked.

Anna reached for the blue cap and gown hanging on the closet door. "What are you wearing underneath, or had you planned to shock everyone, and bare it all?"

"I think it's a little too cool for that kind of self-expression tonight," countered Aileen. "You are confusing me with your twin, Amy?"

The three girls laughed aloud, remembering some of the antics, adventuresome and hot tempered, Amy had pulled off through the years.

Aileen dressed in a lavender poodle skirt, white pullover sweater and black flats, took the cap and gown off the hanger and placed them across her arm.

Heading for the front door, she stopped to take one last look in the full length mirror attached to the back of the closet door. She drew in her stomach and pulled her sweater down at the same time, hoping that her increasing waist line would not be too noticeable.

Corbin, standing on the porch was mumbling something about Ella making them late, and she always waited until the last minute ending with, "That woman, I tell you."

Arriving early proved beneficial. Corbin was able to find a parking space near the entrance to John Logan Bryant High School auditorium. The family of eleven piled out of the 1930 Studebaker. Ella Sumpner stopped to check that everyone looked decent before entering the auditorium.

Standing at the double glass door was a smiling Michael, his blue shirt making his eyes seem an even deeper blue. His smiles broadened at the sight of Aileen. She smiled back and the two holding hands rushed to get to the prep room backstage.

Commencement Exercise was as usual long and boring. Principal Dilworth gave his usual speech of adoration for the support of parents, teachers the school board and Superintendent. The Superintendent gave his speech on the status of the school and what great expectations he had for the Graduating Class of 1933 and the classes to come. Reverend Goodacre, the local minister, spoke again on the benefits of abstinence and something about soaring birds that choose the right highway.

The entire first row of graduates mouthed the words as the Reverend spoke them, having memorized them from the last five or six graduations.

Somewhere in all of this, Ella had to pinch Corbin, eyes closed and mouth open, to wake him before he started to snore. Then finally, the diplomas were issued, the tassels moved to the other side, caps thrown in the air, hugs, kisses, tears (some real and some force), Congratulations!   And it was all over.

Michael and Aileen rushed to find their parents to let them know that they would be driving together to the graduation party at the community center.

Waving good night, as they walked to the Studebaker, Anna whispered to Amy, “Do you think she will tell him?”

“You want something from the kitchen?” Corbin Sumpner asked his wife, turning to get out of bed.

“Hmm, no thanks”, Ella replied.

Making his nightly visit to the kitchen for water, Corbin passed the kids’ rooms and looked in to check, as he had since the first night that he had become a father.

Aileen’s bed, he noticed, had not been slept in. He continued to the kitchen, filled a glass from the faucet, and returned to look in the kids’ room again. No Aileen!

Back in his own bedroom, he gently nudged his wife.

“Did Aileen say she would spend the night with her friends tonight?”

“No, what do you mean?”

“Aileen is not in her room.”

“What do you mean, not in her room?” Ella asked, leaping from the bed grabbing for her pink chenille robe, dipping her feet into her slippers, running to the girls’ room to look.

“What should we do?” ”Should we call Michael’s parents?”

Chapter 6

"How is your momma doing these days? We haven't seen her at the Charity Board Meetings in a while."

David looked up and was surprised to see Bethel standing on her front porch, tin watering can in her hand, pretending to water her plants. Dead ivy leaves clung to dried vines, mossy begonia, soggy verbena and other lifeless plants littered the floor of the screened-in porch.

"Nosy old hen" David said under his breath.

"Oh hello, Cousin Beth, Mama is doing fine." he replied, in the polite way his mother had taught him and expected all of her children to behave.

Bethel Drummond and her husband Henry lived two houses down the street from the Sumpners. Bethel was a double cousin, though no one had as yet been able to explain just how that came to be.

She spent the majority of her time in bed, in the front room of her house, with the door open so that she had a clear view of the street outside, and in ear shot of any conversation near her front yard. Some people believed that she had lip reading abilities. She claimed to be disabled and was attended to by Henry, who always seemed to be within ear shot of her constant barrage of calls. She ate in bed, she drank in bed, she watched television in bed, and she saw her company, including the Women's Charity Board, while in bed.

Bethel was only five feet tall and weighed over two hundred pounds, most of it hips. Today she was wearing a black and grey checkered skirt. Each time she attempted to bend and water a plant, the hem of her skirt rose to expose the back of her fat knees. The fat on her knees resembled two round faces being squeezed then release. She had an average size torso and waist, but below the waist her hips and butt were massive. The weight of her hips and butt made it difficult for her to spend any extended length of time standing. She had short legs, which didn't make matters any better.

And so, long suffering Henry was there to tend to his wife's every need, except on days when he could escape to take care of the needs of some of the single ladies in the neighborhood.

Bethel had earned the well-deserved title of the biggest gossip in the neighborhood. Her business was finding out and spreading everyone else's business. From childhood, Ella Sumpner's children were aware that they were not to discuss personal business in front of or with Nosy Beth.

"Well, what's it been now about two years since Aileen and that Crenshaw boy have been gone? Has she heard anything yet?"

"Cousin Beth, I'm sorry but I have got to get to work. It's almost 3:30 and I have to clock in by 4:00. I will tell Momma that you asked about her. And tell her to give you a call."

"You can expect that call when hell freezes completely over," he thought to himself.

"Your poor momma," Bethel continued murmuring to herself as she continued her watering.

David Sumpner, now eighteen years old, had worked at the Eastplex Sawmill for two years. He had left high school as a senior, after finding out that his girlfriend, Lea, was pregnant.

Eastplex was the main source of employment in the Clover Grove neighborhood. David started working there part-time, during his sophomore year of high school and had walked to work from his parents' home daily since.

He had meet Lea at a community center dance on Valentine's Day nearly a year ago. Lea, tall lean and curvy, was from the high school in the city and did not live in Clover Grove.

His first impression was that she was friendly, a lot friendlier than most of the girls in the Grove. She had walked up to him and a group of his friends and introduced herself. When he said he was going outside to smoke a cigarette, she asked if she could go along.

Once outside she asked if she could have a cigarette too. David didn't know any girls who smoked. He could not think of one girl in Clover Grove who would go outside alone with a boy, for fear of gossip, their parents, and the wrath of God.

He handed her the cigarette and struck a match on the bottom of his shoe heel and lit the cigarette she was holding between her fingers. He looked at her graceful slender smooth hands, her nails painted pink to match her lips. He mentally compared them to the hands of girls he knew, girls who milked cows, carried heavy pails, and slopped hogs, the girls of Clover Grove.

But Lea wasn't like the girls of Clover Grove; she was clever, daring, what the women of the Grove would call fast. He liked that about her. She was willing to try anything. Lea wasn't like any girl he had ever known; she was a buddy, only female.

During their conversation, he found out that she liked to fish, camp, hike any outdoor activity. So when he and a group of guys went fishing at Ferguson Lake, he called to see if she would like to go.

After the fishing trip, David was the last to be dropped off. As they approached his house, he could see Maggie, his girlfriend since eighth grade. A bit chubby for her five foot frame, she was still an attractive girl. She was wearing a red plaid shirt, her blue dungarees rolled up to her ankle, her t strapped flats tapping the floor as she leaned against the pole on the porch. His mother, Ella, was sitting in one of the two large wooden rocking chairs, shelling peas.

"Did you enjoy your trip? Catch anything?" Maggie sarcastically asked.

"Dang, what do you mean by that?" he asked, lifting his prize catch from the back of his friend's truck. His focus was on the story of how he caught the prize bass that he was preparing to share with his father.

"That Lea girl, the one you have been spending so much time with, that's what I mean." Maggie said.

David could tell Maggie was upset, but he was too excited about his catch. He walked pass her into the house in search of his father so that he could show off his catch. Maggie was hot on his heels.

"Did you think I would not find out?"

Ella yelled, "Put those fish in the sink and don't mess up my kitchen floor with the mud on your boots."

"Find out what, Maggie?" "Lea is just a friend. She is just like one of the fellows. She likes to fish, she likes to hunt; you don't like either, and so she went with me and the rest of the guys. And that's all there is to that."

"Maggie, will you stay for dinner?" Ella asked.

"No Miss Sumpner, I had better be getting home."

"Then David will have to give you a ride home; it's getting dark outside."

David dutifully showered, changed clothes and asked his dad for the Studebaker keys. "No need in having two women mad at me." He reasoned.

On the drive home Maggie had softened. She even allowed David to put his right arm around her shoulder as they made the drive to her house.

He walked her to the front door and gave her a gentle kiss on her lips. "Good night," she said.

"See you later," he responded.

He returned to the truck and began the drive home. As he passed the General Store, he noticed someone he thought he recognized. Making a U-turn, he pulled over near the gas pumps to see if his recognition was right. Indeed it was. One lone street light shone over the telephone booth, where she stood.

"Lea, what are you doing out so late? Are you alone?"

"Well, yeah I am alone. I thought I would walk to the store and get cigarettes and be back home before dark. I guess I misjudged the time, or I walked too slowly. Anyway, can you give me a lift home?"

"Sure, jump in."

Lea got in on the passenger side and closed the heavy pale blue Studebaker door.

David began to drive away, and then asked, "By the way, where do you live?"

"Not that far from here, but I was thinking, why don't we go down to the lake and watch the stars for a bit."

David, surprised, nodded his head and steered the car in the direction of Ferguson Lake. David parked the car on a hill overlooking the lake, where they could see the moon and stars reflect off the water like little glints of gold and silver.

They sat on the hood of the car and talked for a bit, and then Lea leaned in and kissed him strong on his lips. Her lips felt soft, warm and moist. She smelled of lavender and jasmine. She took his hand and slid it under her blouse. David began to feel warm all over his body. His breathing deepened and quickened.

"Let's get on the back seat," she whispered.

David feeling a stiffening inside his pants, moved quickly to open the back door and crawl in. Both proceeded to disrobe, waist down. Lea lay on her back and David climbed on top. Clinging together, their bodies moved as one. Sensations David had never felt were bursting all over his body, like tiny fireworks moving all over his skin, up his back, then through his inner thighs. He could hear sounds coming from underneath him, combinations of panting and moaning. His body began to tremble, he gasped, and then it was done.

With Lea's directions David drove her home. He walked her to her door and said goodnight. He walked back to the Studebaker and drove home.

Chapter 7

"Pregnant? How?" David yelled into the telephone, then moved quickly to close the hallway door. "That's not possible. We only did it once. And you can't get pregnant the first time. Are you sure, Lea, are you sure?"

Lea assured David that she was quite sure of her pregnancy, and that she was sure that he was the father.

David had not seen or talked to Lea since the night they had gone to the lake. He thought nothing of the fact that he and Lea had had no contact; after all, they were only friends. They were buddies, who like doing many of the same things.

David paced back and forth down the hallway. "I need to get some air," he said to himself, walking toward the front door. He looked out at the post on the front porch and thought, "Maggie, how do I tell Maggie?"

Another two weeks would pass before David again received a phone call from Lea.

"David, can you come and pick me up at the General Store? I'm really sick and I have no one else to call. Please hurry."

Without asking his father, for fear of having to explain where he was going and why, David sneaked into the kitchen. He took the keys from the wooden key holder that he had made in fifth grade wood shop as a gift for his father. He felt an uneasiness in the pit of his stomach. He felt he was taking a road that would be difficult to come back from. But he was not ready to discuss this with his parents or anybody else, for that matter. If only his older sister Aileen were here, she would understand, and she would know what to do.

David drove up to the General Store and spotted Lea standing on the outside. She was wrapped in an oversized coat, she looked frail.

She walked over to the car and struggled to get in.

“Are you okay?” David asked. “What’s wrong?”

“Can we go somewhere and talk?” Lea asked.

David drove to the park not far from the General Store. He parked the car, and then turned to look at Lea again. Her face was sweaty and so pale that she almost blended into the beige seat covering. Her lips were dry and cracked.

“Lea, what’s wrong?” David asked.

“I tried to get rid of the baby,” Lea stated, whimpering.

“You did what?”

“My friend said she knew how to get rid of the baby. How to make it come out. She said all I needed to do was stick a clothes hanger up there and puncture it, and it would come out as a little blood clot. She said I needed to do it before I was too far along. She said she knew lots of girls who had done it. So I tried it.”

“How long have you been like this?”

“About three days.”

“We need to get you to a doctor.”

“I can’t go to a doctor here. We have to go to the other side of the county where no one will know me. There is a clinic there.”

David turns the car around and headed to First Federal Bank. He withdrew one hundred dollars from his savings account and headed north on Hwy 47.

The doctor who saw Lea said that no damage had been done to the fetus. Lea had however, managed to slightly tear her lower abdominal tissue. She would need antibiotics. She was given a shot and a prescription to fill. She would need to rest until she regained her strength.

The doctor further warned her that attempting to abort a child was illegal and could have resulted in her going to jail.

On the drive home, David turned to Lea and asked, “Is the baby mine?”

Lea responded, “I’m sure this baby is yours.”

“Then I will honor my responsibility as a man. I will ask your parents to allow us to be married,” David pledged.

Lea laid her head on David’s shoulder and slept the rest of the way home.

“How do I tell Maggie?” rang over and over in David head as he drove home.

It was dark when David pulled the Studebaker into the car shed. He was too dazed to attempt an explanation of why he had taken the car without permission.

He took a minute to look up at the stars and thought what a beautiful night for so much trouble.

David walked into the back door and entered the kitchen. He placed the car key back on the brown wooden key holder and headed to the front room where he knew his mother and father would be waiting.

"Might as well get this over with," he thought.

Ella was sitting in her chair near the fireplace, various hues of knitting yarn spread across her lap.

Corbin was sitting in his favorite high-back chair, reading the bible. David sat on Ella's cherished pink velvet settee situated between the chairs of his parents.

He put his hands together and looked down at the small circular rug on the floor, contemplating, searching for the right words, the right phrase to start off with. Nothing came to his mind. No words, no phrases!

Finally, Corbin spoke, "You got something to tell me, son?"

David looked up at his father, "Dad, I'm in trouble."

Sensing that this was a son to father conversation, Ella gathered her knitting and put it into the wicker basket on the floor. She stood, smoothed her skirt, and started to leave the room.

"Momma, I think you need to hear this too."

"No son, you and your dad talk this out and then I will hear about it later," she said as she walked out into the hallway toward her bedroom.

"Ah, ah, ah she said, she said, she said… she is pregnant and that I am the father."

"Maggie is pregnant," Corbin said, almost in a shriek.

At first David did not clearly understand what his father had said. The words rushed by his ears but did not register. He was not prepared for that response. Then realizing what his father had said.

He corrected his father, “No dad, not Maggie. Lea, Lea is pregnant.”

“Who the hell is Lea?” Corbin asked.

David, now sitting in his mother’s chair directly in front of his father, began to cry as he told his father about Lea. Weeping, he told about the attempted abortion, the trip to the clinic and his promise to marry Lea.

His father took his son by the shoulders, looked him in his eyes and said, “Son, it has always been our hope, your mom and mine, that we would raise responsible men and women. It honors me that you are a responsible young man. I am proud that you want to take ownership and marry the mother of your child. I won’t kid you. You are only seventeen years old and being a father at your age will not be easy. Your mother and I will always love you and support you in your decision.”

He lifted his son to his feet, hugged him, both with tears on their cheeks. “Now go to bed son, I will talk with your mom. Tomorrow we will go together to speak to Lea’s parents.”

Corbin and Ella had expected their children to be responsible for their actions and it was with this characteristic that David had made his plan to tell Maggie about the pregnancy. He would speak to her and her parents at the same time. He would explain how this happened and let them know that he had never planned to hurt Maggie or string her along.

However, this meeting would never take place. Someone had made sure that Maggie knew only a few days after David himself had found out.

The envelope was laying address side up on the front porch. Addressed to Mr. David Paul Sumpner

To: Mr. David Sumpner,

It is apparent that the five years we spent together meant nothing to you. I am sorry to have wasted your time. Not to mention the time I wasted.

You could have been man enough to tell me yourself, instead of having one of your friends call and tell my mother. Of course, she was devastated. Both of my parents had trusted you as much as I have. I can't begin to tell you how foolish you have made me feel.

I never thought you would do this to me. I thought that I meant more to you. All the promises you made about getting married once we finished high school! The plans we had for prom! You know that my mom has already made my prom dress, so now what am I supposed to do with it?

Worse yet is when I asked you about that girl, you lied to my face. And I believed it all. All I can say is I hope you will be happy in your new life.

Sincerely

Maggie

PS. I never want to see you again. Please do not attempt to contact me. !!!!!!!Father!!!!!!!!.

Chapter 8

"Ella, come on the boy and me are ready," Corbin yelled down the hallway. "That woman takes all day to get ready, I tell you."

Minutes later, a flustered Ella, entered the room, wearing her green jewel neckline dress with scallop edging, beige ankle strapped pumps and carrying a beige clutch handbag. Her pillbox beige hat crowned her dark red hair which was pulled back in a bun. "Okay, I'm ready, let's go."

Ella Sumpner at 37 years old still had the youthful body of the seventeen year old who married Corbin Paul Sumpner twenty years ago. At five foot nine inches tall, her clear skin, high etched cheek bones, exotic brown eyes, beautiful full lips and shoulder length reddish brown hair, still caused men to take a second look when she walked by.

Corbin suggested that David drive since he knew where they were going.

David started the car drove down the black tar road to Hwy 47, passed the General Store, Main Street downtown, and into a community unlike Clover Grove. It lacked the stability of Clover Grove. There was street after street of building with rental signs in the window. People were standing aimlessly on street corners and outside of seedy cafes'.

Ella was glad she had gotten into the back seat. She was sure that if David saw her now, he would be able to read the sense of uneasiness on her face.

David parked on the street in front of a greyish blue building. The three got out of the car and approached one of the two broken and cracked sidewalks. The white numbers on the side of the door read 10A.

David knocked on the door and Lea opened the door. The repulsive smell of years of smoke and alcohol washed over them at the door.

“Hello,” Lea said, forcing a half smile.

” Come in. Have a seat,” she continued, pointing to the sofa.

Ella looked over at the sofa and thought about the dog pallet she had made when Susie, their black lab had given birth to pups. She fought to bend her knee and sit, folding her beautiful satin green dress under her.

“This is my mom, Claudia” Lea said, pointing to the youngish looking woman, standing in the hallway door. Her reddish blonde hair was pulled back into a pony tail. Holding a cigarette between the fingers of one hand, Claudia crossed the room and used the free hand to shake hands with Ella, then Corbin.

“Isn’t your father going to join us? “Ella inquired.

“Lea’s father is not here. He is in the state hospital in Jacksonville.” replied Claudia. “He had a crisis.”

Ella took a small white kerchief from her purse. She dabbed beneath her eyes, attempting to hide the look of dismay on her face. She knew that state hospital was a gentle way of saying mental institution.

The pregnancy was discussed and plans for the wedding, next Sunday after church at the Sumpner's home. Small family gathering, afterward the couple would live with Ella and Corbin until they were able to afford their own place.

Arrangements were made in the Sumpner house for the new couple: a cot in the living room for one boy, a bed in the small room in back that Ella used for canning would be sufficient for the other boy, and the new couple could have the boys' room off the kitchen. The four girls would keep their room, since there were already two sets of bunk beds, and the baby girl's bed would be moved back into the Ella and Corbin's room.

"It will be a tight fit, but we will make it work, "Ella contemplated.

Chapter 9

Reverend Goodacre arrived thirty minutes early, as was his way. This would give him time to settle payment arrangement before the wedding began, in case, for some reason, the wedding did not actually take place. He wanted to ensure that his expenses were covered.

"Understanding is a good thing," he liked to say.

All the Sumpner girls: five-year-old Grace, seven-year-old Dana, nine-year-old Lorraine and the 14-year-old twins were dressed in identical pink dresses to match their mother's, white stockings and black patent leather shoes. Ella had sewn almost nonstop for three days to complete all the dresses.

Corbin and the boys wore white shirts and black slacks.

The twins at the piano attempted to play Mendelssohn's Wedding March and only partly mangled it, considering the 6 months of piano lessons between them.

Lea entered the room and she was beautiful, her long hair had been pulled atop her head in a bun, golden curls framed her face. The hem of the beautiful white wedding dress that Ella had loaned her flowed across the floor as she walked to stand next to David.

Lea's mother, Claudia, blushed as she saw her daughter, more beautiful than she had ever seen her.

After Reverend Goodacre pronounced, "You are now husband and wife. You may now kiss the bride." David leaned forward and kissed Lea on her cheek. They then turned to greet their guests.

And so the Sumpners' household of ten again became eleven, with one due in approximately eight months.

After the wedding, the new couple moved into their room, and the house began the journey back toward normalcy.

Ella went about her days, getting to know her new daughter-in-law. One thing she noticed immediately was that Lea knew very little about housework, cooking, gardening or animals.

She did notice though that Lea was a very anxious learner. Lea enjoyed the chores that she was assigned and was willing to do even more. It wasn't long before Lea had fit in just like another daughter.

She especially enjoyed time spent in the kitchen learning to cook new meals. After only a few failed attempts, she was able to make biscuits almost as good as Ella. And Ella had even said so.

The women of the house sang as they cleaned, cooked, knitted and mended. Lea was happier than she had ever been. This was a family like she had never known. She enjoyed the interaction within the family. She enjoyed sitting at a dinner table filled with the noise of the day's activities. Lea had only vague memories of her grandparents. She had seen her own father twice in her life that she could remember.

In this house, she felt accepted and welcome, and she thought loved.

Each night Lea and the twins set about knitting for the new baby. Anna was knitting blankets, one blue and one pink, Amy booties one set blue and one pink, and Lea new at knitting, was trying her hand at making a tiny sweater.

Sitting in his chair reading his bible, as usual, Corbin was surrounded by the chatter of women making plans for the new baby. He himself had been hiding out in the shed busy making a surprise baby crib. The house was abuzz with the joy that new life brings.

One evening after the chores were done; the girls were sitting on the porch looking up at the sky, trying to see faces in the stars. Lea was sitting in one of the big rockers and the twins were lying on the porch with their legs swinging off the edge.

Anna looked over and saw water under Lea's chair. "Lea you peed on yourself," she said.

Looking under the rocker, Lea replied, "Oh my God, get mama."

Anna ran into the house screaming, "Mama, Mama, Lea wants you."

"What is it?" Ella asked.

"Lea is on the porch and she is sitting in pee."

Ella realizing the urgency, yelled to Corbin," Go and get Mrs. Whitman."

"Mrs. Who?"

"Mrs. Whitman man, the Midwife, we are about to have a baby!"

Once Mrs. Whitman arrived, the delivery went smoothly. David, who was working at the mill, missed the delivery. He came home that evening to a beautiful little girl with long thick brown eyelashes that curled almost back to their lids. Her head was crowned with a mass of thick brown curls. "She," he thought, "was prefect."

Holding her in his arms for the first time, he kissed her tiny hand. Her tiny fingers curled around one of his. He thought to himself, “I will protect you with my life.”

Silently, he promised that he would try to be at least as good at fathering as his dad had been to him. He would work to provide for all her needs. He was in love the moment he laid eyes on this beautiful bundle in her pink, knitted blanket.

Chapter 10

The sound was so violent it refused to go unheard. It shook the dishes from the cupboard, it shook the barns, it forced the hens off the perches, it caused the horses to rear, and the cows to run senselessly in all directions, and it shook the very earth.

It caused every mother, every father, every wife, and every child in Clover Grove to look toward Farm Road 1127 in absolute shock and fear. The tall timbers swayed and then there was smoke, on Farm Road 1127, which lead to Eastplex Sawmill.

At the school the principal announced that all students were to be kept in their classrooms, arms covering their heads and under their desk until further notice.

Some families got into their cars to drive to the mill, some went by wagon or horseback and some people just began to run toward FM 1127, unable to reason that it would take longer to get there by foot. The road filled with people trying to get to the mill as fast as they could.

Corbin was in the Studebaker; Ella opened the door to get in. Corbin told her to wait until he could get information. Someone needed to stay home and wait for the children to come in from school. Reluctantly, Ella agreed.

Lea stood on the porch, mouth open and eyes fixed on the cloud of smoke rising above the tall timbers of FM 1127.

Corbin drove as far as he could, huge logs laid across the road. He got out of the car and continued on foot. At the gates that lead to the mill, he recognized Peter Crenshaw. Peter Crenshaw, Michael's father, was attempting to organize the men into rescue teams. Corbin stepped over broken branches and bits of machinery and other litter to get to Peter.

“Have you seen David?” He asked Peter.

Peter looked at a handwritten roster in his hand.

“David, David has gone to the hospital.” “Memorial.”

Leaping over huge fallen trees and other debris, Corbin ran back to his car, and drove to the hospital.

When Corbin arrived at the hospital, the Sheriff Deputies were stationed at the entrance to the emergency room area. Families stood crowding the steps outside, in the hallways, in the waiting room area, and in every available space.

“I want to see my son,” Corbin shouted. The deputies tried to get him to wait until the doctor could come out to speak to him.

“I want to see my son,” Corbin shouted, pushing aside the deputies. Dr. Kincaid, hearing the noise in the hallway came out to speak to Corbin.” He wants to see you,” the doctor said.

Corbin walked to the bed side. He didn’t recognize his son. There were bandages covering almost his entire face. David reached out his scorched hand so blistered it was hard to recognize it as a hand, and his father gently laid his fingers on it.

“Dad, promise me you will take care of my daughter. Promise me, Dad. Promise me.”

Corbin could barely speak. He choked out the word, “Son, it’s going to be alright. You will be alright, Son.”

"Dad, promise me."

"You know that I will, son. You know that I will. But things are going to be alright. You will be alright," Corbin said, trying to convince himself as well as his son.

Dr. Kincaid had known the Sumpner family for three generations. He was the only doctor for miles. He had tended the Sumpner clan through measles, chicken pox, and various other childhood diseases, scrapes and broken bones. He walked over to Corbin and whispered, "Can I talk to you outside?" Putting his arm around Corbin shoulder the two men walked in shared pain, into the hallway.

"Corbin, I don't think he will make it through the night. We have given him all the pain medication that his body can take, but that will not be enough to stop the pain. We just hope he will be able to sleep. We will do all we can but, he is burned over eighty percent of his body. I am surprised that he has lasted this long."

At this, Corbin had to reach for the side of the wall to hold himself up. He wanted to hit something, somebody. He looked into Dr. Kincaid's face and saw that the doctor too was hurting.

"Have you spoken to Ella, does she know?" questioned Dr. Kincaid.

Dr. Kincaid! Dr. Kincaid! Dr. Kincaid! The nursing staff was calling from all directions.

This was the first time that he had thought about Ella's need to know.

"Ella, Ella needs to know."

Corbin slowly allowed his knees to bend and sat on the floor outside his son's room, contemplating. "Ella needs to know." But not now, she can't see her son like this. I will call her, but not now. He put his face into his hands and wept, like he had never wept before. With no cares for where he was, or who saw him, He wept.

He took his handkerchief from the side pocket of his coveralls and wiped his face. Using the wall behind him for support, Corbin straightened himself, stood and walked back to his son's bedside. He lifted the bible which lay on the table next to the bed. Looking down at the unopened bible, he held in his hand, he began a prayful whisper, "The Lord is my shepherd, I shall not want."

Stumbling to remember the verses to follow, he repeated, "The Lord is my Shepherd, I shall not want." He maketh me to lie down in green pastures." He hadn't realized but his voice has grown louder and stronger and more forceful. Busy nurses, other families, and other hospital staff had joined in, "He leaded me beside the still waters. He restoreth my soul: He…." Suddenly the entire emergency room had become one in prayer. "Leadeth me in the paths of righteousness for his name's sake"

Corbin looked at his son's face, eyes swollen shut. David was attempting to mouth the words "Yea, though I walk through the valley of the shadow of death, I will fear no evil: for thou art with me; thy rod and thy staff they comfort me."

David's lips dry and chapped continued in unison with his father. "Thou preparest a table before me in the presence of mine enemies: thou anointest my head with oil; my cup runneth over. Surely goodness and mercy shall follow me all the days of my life: and I will dwell in the house of the Lord forever."

And then it was done. Corbin leaned over and kissed his son on his bandaged forehead and whispered, "I love you my son."

Dr. Kincaid, standing over David's body, declared that his life ended at 5:46 pm., Wednesday, June 3, 1935.

The local newspaper article read:

Thursday, June 4, 1935

Three men perished in an explosion at the Eastplex Sawmill on Wednesday, and 23 men were seriously injured.

Thomas Frasier 33, a husband and father of four, had worked at the mill for over 16 years.

Theodore Massing 42, husband and father of 6 children and three grandchildren, had worked at the mill for 22 years.

David Paul Sumpner 19, husband and father of 1 child, had worked at the mill for 4 years.

Several workers who refused to be identified told our reporter about dangerous working conditions at the mill. Workers had been complaining to supervisors and management that they felt the steam boiler was unsafe. However a representative for Eastplex, Peter Crenshaw stated that employee safety is always the company's paramount concern. The company is extremely saddened by the loss of life and the injury to employees. And the families have the management's deepest sympathy.

The truth:

The Great Depression had been hard on all businesses. The mill had only been operational sporadically for much of the past three years. Company management was aware that the steam boiler needed to be replaced. Eastplex, like many other small companies, throughout the nation, was waiting for federal funds from the Emergency Banking

Act to be distributed to states and funneled through the banks to businesses.

The funeral was held at the First Baptist Church on Main Street. Ella felt a rush of appreciation as the family limousine approached the church. There were cars and horse-drawn wagons parked on both sides of the street for as far as it was possible to see. "All these people are here for my son," to herself she sighed.

Reverend Goodacre was waiting at the chapel door. And so the family lined up, Lea and the baby in matching yellow dresses, with white lace collars, then Corbin and Ella, followed by the rest of the children and other family members.

The girls all dressed in white, Ella has proclaimed that no one was to wear black. This was a celebration of the life of her wonderful, loving, fun-loving, talented and energetic son. And no one was to dishonor his life; the service was to reflect the life he had lived.

Inside First Baptist Church, the largest church of any denomination in the city, every pew was filled. Crowds of people stood against the walls and in the aisle, through the doors and spilled out into the courtyard. The usher board did its best to direct traffic but was soon overwhelmed.

Reverend Goodacre rose to begin officiating, taking the ever-present handkerchief from his front pocket, he wiped at the sweat that always seemed to seep into the folds at the back of his fat neck. Even with all the windows open, the temperature inside the church was stifling.

Mrs. Fisher, David's counselor spoke about how determined David was as a student at John Logan Bryant High, the great potential he demonstrated for art, and that he would have one day been a great artist.

Several neighbors spoke of how respectful David was and how he was always willing to give a helping hand.

David's friends spoke about how David could not resist a triple dare, a double dare maybe, but a triple no way. Like when they were five-year-olds and had snuck into the cow pasture at midnight, to prove that cows slept standing up. They heard a strange noise and every one of them ran into the barbed wire fence. The result was a trip to Dr. Kincaid's office. A prank that ended in a good chewing out, as well as, a good spanking for each of them, for being outside without supervision at midnight.

Ella looked down the pew to see her children's faces covered in tears. She wanted so to go to them and comfort them. In her own sorrow, she could not find the strength.

Reverend Goodacre read from the book 1 Thessalonians 4:13-14

Brothers, we do not want you to be ignorant about those who fall asleep, or to grieve like the rest of men, who have no hope. We believe that Jesus died and rose again and so we believe that God will bring with Jesus those who have fallen asleep in him.

He recalled speaking to David on the day of his wedding. He spoke of how David had been reared in the church and David though a young man, had developed a close relationship with God, the Father.

He recalled the time that David drank the communion wine then filled the decanters with red Kool aide.

He assured Corbin, Ella, and David's young wife, that one day they would see David again.

"The Lord giveth and the Lord taketh away."

The organist began the Recessional. The Reverend stood and walked to the front of the casket to lead the procession.

Ella stood and tried to make a step. She was unable to move. She looked down at her feet in confusion. Her mind was telling her body to move, but her body didn't obey. She was trying with all her might to make her feet move, yet they resisted. Every inch of her body wanted to run, to sprint, to race, to catch up with the wooden box carrying her baby.

Finally, she felt one foot slide forward. From some distant place, she watched herself, as she began to fall toward the floor. Her knees would not hold her body, they wobbled like jello. She felt herself going down. Somewhere in the deep vortex which had separated her body from her mind, she felt Corbin's arms around her waist, as he lifted her to his chest.

"I've got you, baby." He whispered, "I've got you." "I'll never let you go."

Together, they made their way down the pew lined aisle, through the door, to the waiting limousine parked behind the hearse, which carried their son, "Ella's baby".

Chapter 11

No one knew where Aileen and Michael were and, therefore, could not reach them with information about funeral arrangements for David. Ella felt that she had lost two children and she could not understand why she was being so punished.

For months, Ella found it impossible to find the energy to get out of bed. The family was left to survive on the mounds and mounds of food delivered by neighbors. There were cakes, pies, baked, broiled and fried chicken, ham, casseroles of all sorts covering every kitchen countertop, as well as the dinner table.

Anna and Amy went about trying to care for the younger children and provide meals for their father. Corbin was spending more and more time in the fields and in the car shed where he worked to repair farm equipment for farmers in the community.

The twins, giving up on getting Ella to come to the table for meals, had started taking her meals into her bedroom. One day as Ella laid in her bed looking out the open window, watching the wind blow the blue linen window panels, there was the slightest knock at her bedroom door.

"Come in," Ella said weakly. "Who is it?"

"Me, I hungry,"

Ella jumped from the bed, and ran to the door. Sitting outside the bedroom door was her bright eyed grandbaby wearing a periwinkle dress with syrup stains down the front an undone bow hanging loosely from her hair onto her face. It was Lilla.

Lilla, which means Little One in Swedish, is the name David had given his daughter. Sweden was the first place David had planned to take his daughter when she was old enough and he had earned enough money to travel there. He had wanted to travel to Sweden since reading about the paintings of Alexander Roslin, whose work was considered playful and witty, character traits David thought he too possessed.

Ella stooped to pick up her grandbaby. “Where is everybody and why haven’t you eaten.” Walking through the house, Ella surmised that the children had all gone to school. But where was Lea?

Ella tapped on the bedroom door of the room that had been shared by David and Lea. No answer, the door was partially open. Ella peered in. The baby’s clothing, shoes, Lea’s clothing were scattered all over the floor. David’s clothes were neatly arranged on the bed, with gentle folds here and there. It appeared that Lea and the baby had been sleeping atop all of David’s clothing.

Ella searched the house, then the barns, the back yard and the car shed, where Corbin was working bent over one of the many tractors lined up for repair in the back yard.

“Have you seen Lea?” Ella asked. “The baby was in the house alone. And there is no sign of Lea anywhere.”

Corbin responded that he had not seen Lea all day, but that he had been in the shed since morning when the school bus had come to pick up the children.

Ella returned to the kitchen and began to prepare food for the baby. She then gave the baby a good bath in the kitchen sink and changed her clothes. After feeding the baby she put her down for a nap. She went to the hallway, picked up the telephone and asked the operator to call Claudia Anderson.

Corbin on his nightly trips to the kitchen for water, had watched night after night, as Lea sat in the big rocker on the porch, rocking back and forward and staring at nothing in particular.

The entire house in their own state of grief had ignored the changes in Lea: how she had lost interest in learning to cook, or knit, chores, or how inattentive she had become toward Lilla.

No one noticed, that her eyes seemed glazed, as she moved robotically through the days following the accident.

No one noticed, that she no longer ate or slept, and instead walked through the house and the yard at all hours of the day and night.

No one noticed, that she moved unhearing through a house filled with the noise of the daily lives of eleven people.

No one noticed, that she had begun to mindlessly murmur to herself as she sat in the chair near the window.

No one noticed, the tic that had slowly developed at the corner of her lip just below her right cheek.

No one noticed, the thinning hair, as she wrapped her fingers around one strand after another, pulled it from its follicle and let it fall to the floor.

No one noticed.

Lea would walk to the end of the black tar road where it intersected with Hwy 47. She would stand there, next to the rows of black metal mailboxes, which stood like soldiers waiting for mail call. She would look toward FM 1127 for hours on end. She would stand and look down the road. At first she would stand there for an hour or two then she would return home. Lately, she had started staying from morning until after dark.

And then one day, she just did not return home.

"Claudia, have you heard from Lea today?" Ella asked, trying not to seem too concerned, so as not to disturb Claudia unnecessarily.

"No, not today, not in over a week, I'd say. Why? Is she alright, is Lilla alright."

Ella went on to explain about the condition in which she had found Lilla as well as the condition of Lea's bedroom.

"I'll be over as soon as I can. I have to work until two o'clock today and then I will be right over." Claudia assured.

The family put up missing person posters, and Ella, Corbin and Claudia filed a missing person report with the police, but no one had heard anything. There was an article written in the local newspaper, but no one had heard or seen anything of Lea.

The three grandparents decided that Lilla would remain in Ella and Corbin's care, since it was the only home that she had ever known.

Chapter 12

In the three years since the accident at the mill there had been little reason for joy in the Sumpner household three years old Lilla set in the middle of the kitchen floor surrounded by her aunts, six year old Grace, eight year old Dana, and 11 year old Lorraine.

Lilla, deeply engaged in activity, was learning how to count to 20.

Ella loved and adored every inch of the child. She was her first and only grandchild and all that she had of her son, David. Unknowingly, she would find herself looking for some resemblance to David when she looked at Lilla. She searched for his sandy, sun-bleached hair, which he always wore neatly cropped in a crewcut, his dazzling blue eyes, which seem to grow darker, when he was in a game of mischief. She searched but she did not find him.

"Beautiful child," she thought, "There is plenty of time for her to grow and change," she said, patting the top of Lilla's thick, dark curls. Lilla looked up at her grandmother with her deep brown eyes and long dark eyelashes and smiled.

Outside Ella heard the banging of a ball being thrown against the house.

"Lorraine, tell those boys to stop bouncing that ball against the house. Wish they had never discovered that dang basketball game." Ella shouted. "Tell them to go get the mail from the mailbox. That should use up some of that energy."

She heard the sprinting and shuffling of teenage boys, running to see who could be first to get to the mailbox at the end of the road and back.

“Hugh, Carlton, you boys be careful near that highway, those cars come over that hill really fast, nowadays”, Ella warned. “Stay off that highway. There is no reason for you to even be on the highway. Do you boys hear me?”

Racing back from the mailbox, down the black tar road, almost neck and neck, the two boys jumped over the steps that lead to the porch and ran into the house.

“It’s a letter from Aileen. Mama, a letter from Aileen.”

Ella dropped to the chair at the kitchen table. Placing her hand on the edge of the table for support, she took the envelope with her other hand. Her hands were shaking so that she could barely hold on to the envelope.

“Let me open it, Mama,” offered Carlton.

“No, Mama let me.” Hugh protested.

“I can open it myself,” she said. “Get your father.”

Dear Momma and Daddy,

I have missed you and my brothers and sisters so much.

I read about David’s accident in the newspaper.

I know you miss him terribly, as do I.

I read that David had gotten married and had a child. I am so happy at the prospect of getting to meet his wife and baby.

I have so much to tell you, so much catching up to do.

I Will be coming home soon, can't wait to see you.

Love,

Your Aileen

"She's coming home," Ella cried, looking up at Corbin." She is coming home."

For the next two weeks, the house was in a state of cleaning: cleaning the floors, the walls, the curtains, the rugs, anything that could not move of its own free will was guaranteed to be cleaned.

Anna and Amy had cleaned Lea and David's room from top to bottom, and still Ella was not pleased, fussing as she took her own mother's white medallion matelassé bedspread from the hope chest at the foot of her bed. She spread it across the bed which would now hold her returning daughter.

Busily checking the canning, to make sure she had pickled apples, Aileen's favorite, Ella heard herself humming. At long last, the house was again alive.

She did not question why Aileen left or where she had been. She was just happy to know her child would be coming home.

Corbin and the boys would drive over to the Southern Pacific Railway Station, platform 3 at 1:30pm on Friday this week. The very thought took Ella's breath away.

There would be a small party Friday evening, just family and close friends, to welcome Aileen home. The house spotless, Ella and the girls set about cooking for the party. “Aileen loves lemon cake, roast beef, baked chicken, and lentil soup with potatoes,” Ella mused. Once again there was singing in the house. “Corbin I need sugar and flour; we have to go to the General Store.”

Finally Friday, Corbin, Hugh and Carlton stood on platform 3 at precisely 1pm. The three men, long necks and legs stretched to their full length, looked like a gruiformes of cranes, as they strained to look down the railroad tracks, to see if they could spot the train which would be carrying Aileen.

An hour passed, then another, it was now 3pm; the three men had resolved to sit on the bench outside the railway station door. Suddenly there was the tw-e-e-e-e-t of a steam whistle, and the rails shook. The three jumped to their feet almost simultaneously. Noticing this, the three laughed. The wait was almost over.

The train, shiny and sleek pulled into the station. The conductor, adorned in a navy blue uniform, dismounted and started to help the passengers to dismount.

A passenger dressed in a brown suit stood in the door. He looked left and then right and finally stepped down from the door. Each passenger seemed to take forever to dismount. Two well -dressed men dismounted, followed by a short round woman, who was struggling to get through the door.

Then, standing in the doorway, was a very fashionably dressed young woman of twenty or so. She wore a heather-grey flannel two piece suit with a pink and gray stripped blouse underneath and grey python and suede lace up pumps.

She looked stunning. Her shocking red hair was pinned under a grey Florentine hat with a round half-brim trimmed in pink. She was holding the hand of a very debonair little boy.

“That’s Aileen,” shouted Hugh, waving. “Aileen. Aileen!”

The three ran toward the train door. Corbin grabbed his daughter off her feet and swung her around in the air. Her hat flew off of her head and her long red hair fell onto her shoulders.

“My girl,” he said. “My Aileen is home.” Kissing her on her cheek and returning her to her feet, only then did he notice that she was not alone.

Looking at the young boy, who had frightfully grabbed her hand, Aileen stated, “Dad, this is Quinn, my son, your grandson.”

Corbin, trying to hide the look of shock on his face, managed a slight smile.

“Quinn, say hello to your Grandfather.”

The young boy stepped forward and lifted his right hand to shake Corbin’s hand. “Hello, sir. I am glad to meet you.” He said.

Stunned, Corbin didn’t quite know what to say, “Hello, son, I am glad to meet you too.”

Hugh and Carlton, jostling for position, both stuck out their hands. Quinn shook hands with both of them, one after the other.

“These are your uncles, Quinn. This is Uncle Hugh and this is Uncle Carlton.”

“We’d better get your luggage. Your mom is anxious for us to get home. Our assignment was to get here and get back as soon as possible. And the last thing I want to do is get on your mom’s bad side." Corbin said, already walking toward the luggage compartment.

Hugh and Carlton carried the steamer trunk to the Studebaker. Using a rope and quite a bit of effort, they secured it onto the rear of the car. Aileen carried her Gladstone bag, and Corbin carried other pieces of luggage.

"I can help," called Quinn, running to retrieve a small bag dropped by his grandfather.

"Indeed, you can," responded Corbin.

The drive home was filled with memories of past events of childhood, laughter, and even songs filled the hour long drive back to Clover Grove.

Turning off Hwy 47 onto the black tar covered street, Aileen could see the Sumpners house on the hill. "Aaah, home," she said, "home."

Opening the car door and stepping onto the gravel covered driveway, Aileen could hear laughter, music and conversations coming from inside. The Sumpner house was overflowing with people, food and happiness.

As soon as Aileen stepped inside the front door, she was met with a stampede of family, neighbors and friends. She was being hugged from all sides; her siblings, friends, but where is Mama, she thought.

Finally she glanced at the door next to the kitchen and there in her favorite pink, tulip covered apron, stood Mama. She stood hands together at her face, as if in disbelief. Tears formed in the corners of Ella's eyes, as Aileen crossed the floor to get to her mom.

Aileen and Ella embraced as if to wash away millions of years of separation. Embarrassed for having made such a scene, Ella wiped her face on her apron and said, “Okay, everybody, let’s get something to eat.”

Having been lost in all the hugging, Quinn raced to his mother’s side and took her hand. Ella looked down at the well-dressed little boy and thought, “What beautiful green eyes.”

“Oh, mom, everybody, this is my son, Quinn.”

Hearing this, Carol and her mom, Jennifer broke through the crowd. Jennifer reached down and swept the child into her arms, hugging him so intensely that Quinn started to tear.

“Mom,” Carol said, “you are hurting him; you are holding him too tightly.”

Jennifer released the boy and handed him over to Aileen. Quinn, peeling away his mother’s hand, slid down and stood on the floor.

Aileen stooped to face Quinn and said, “Quinn, this is your father’s mother, Grandmother Jennifer. And this is your Aunt Carol. She is your father’s sister.”

Speaking softly she continued. “Remember how we talked about grandparents and I told you that you were a lucky boy because you have four grandparents?”

“Where is Mr. Crenshaw?” asked Aileen. Peter Crenshaw had been invited but had chosen not to attend.

“He couldn’t make it. He said he had work he needed to complete tonight.”

“And Michael” asked, Jennifer,” is Michael here, is he coming?”

Aileen went on to explain that Michael was well and that a business trip to Spain had prevented him from coming with them this trip. However, he would surely be home soon.

In the corner of the room, Carlton had turned on the new Victrola and Lilla was trying to teach her new cousin, Quinn how to dance, while Duke Ellington wailed, “It Don’t Mean a Thing if you Ain’t Got that Swing”. Soon everyone had joined in the dancing, even Corbin gave it a try, spinning Ella ‘round and ‘round the dance floor.

Reverend Goodacre, who had begun snacking as soon as he had entered the front door, was standing guard at the table refilling his plate and trying not to bump any dancers in the process.

After hours of laughter, food and general joy, the guests said their goodnights and left down the black tar road.

Ella, tired from the day’s events, went to her bedroom to rest before starting the chore of cleaning and reorganizing.

The girls, however, still filled with energy and questions for Aileen, went about doing the cleaning. While Dana, Grace and Lorraine went about cleaning the front room, Anna, Amy and Aileen went to the kitchen.

In the front room, Quinn found himself surrounded by his young aunts and baby cousin interrogating him about his life, “Where do you live, how old are you, do you go to school, do you have any sisters and brothers?”

In the kitchen, his mother, Aileen was going through a similar interrogative process.

“So what happened, where have you been?”

Aileen sat down to start the story, beginning with Commencement Night.

Chapter 13

The young man who always had a plan, had absolutely no plan on the night of his commencement exercise five years earlier. He and his girlfriend, Aileen had gotten into his truck to drive to the graduation dance at the community center.

Instead of driving directly to the center however, he drove to the nearby park. He had something special to talk to Aileen about. He parked the truck and turned to Aileen.

“I have something that I want to ask you. We have been together for the past four years. I have never wanted to be with anyone else. My grandfather always said to be sure before you make a lifetime commitment. Of this I am sure, I want to spend the rest of my life with you.”

Taking the small black box from his jacket pocket, he opened it to show the golden band with the small diamond in its center. “Will you marry me?” he asked.

Looking down at her hands in her lap, “I… I…. I can’t,” Aileen replied,

Not the answer Michael had expected, he shook his head to make sure that he heard her right.

“I don’t understand. You can’t!” Michael was looking in Aileen’s face searching for some reasoning. Some reason for this answer. Somewhere between his ears the word ‘can’t’ was echoing, as if he was searching for the meaning of the word.

"I thought you wanted to marry me," fighting to get the words out of his stomach.

"I did…..I mean…I do…but"

"But, but, but what. Four years Aileen, four years and now, all you can say is but," Michael said through tears, almost shouting.

Aileen, crying at this point, said, "Michael, there is something I have to tell you." She then told him the entire story of how she had gone to the hen house and had been ambushed by three men and raped by one of them. She swore him to secrecy; she told him that only her twin sisters knew of the rape. Her father, she begged, was never to know.

Michael was at first angry with Aileen, then with himself, then angry with the three men who had caused such brutal damage to Aileen. He reached over and took Aileen into his arms." I'm so sorry, he said, "I'm so sorry!"

"Michael, I'm pregnant," She said, weeping into his shoulder. "I know how this changes everything. I understand that you can't marry me now." The tears flooding down her cheeks into her mouth caused the words to bubble from her lips. "I have loved you my entire life. I don't want you to be hurt. I only want you to be happy in your life. That's why I can't marry you."

They sat together in silence for what seemed an eternity. Michael pulled her over to him, kissed her gently on her lips and cradled her as she lay crying on his shoulder.

Sitting in the dark of the truck, Michael thought about his plans. He thought about the horses, the small house, and the land. The land his grandfather had once owned, and that he had planned one day to own.

While Aileen lay sleeping, he thought.

Aileen awoke to find Michael driving away from the First Federal Bank, headed north on highway 47. Exhausted she lay her head on Michael's shoulder and went back to sleep.

The wrenching of the trucks brakes startled Aileen awake. Looking out the window, she noticed a banner hanging by the door of the wooden framed house JC Worthrop, Justice of the Peace.

"Come with me," Michael said.

The ceremony only lasted a few minutes and they were now Mr. and Mrs. Michael Crenshaw.

In the truck again, they headed north.

It was night when they pulled under the neon sign "Ames Travel Court" and parked. Michael went in to make the arrangements. Key in hand, he returned, started the truck and drove pass the rows of small cottages, parking in front of number 12.

Aileen followed him inside. Stopping in the middle of the room, she looked around. At the window, next to the front door, there hung green and red striped curtains. A green rug with tiny red stars covered the entirety of the floor, except for the small kitchenette recessed in a nook near the back door. At the very front corner a full size bed was pushed against another window, with curtain to match the others.

Aileen sat on the end of the bed, which was covered with a green bedspread with bands of red across the bottom to match the striped curtains.

"Get some rest, I'll be right back," Michael said. Too tired from the hours of traveling, Aileen did not protest.

As Michael closed the door behind him, she pulled the covers back, lay her head on the pillows and went to sleep. For the first time in weeks, she slept without being haunted by dreams of that awful night. She had no idea how long she slept but awoke to the sound of keys in the lock outside. She immediately sprang up. She looked around and for a few minutes, didn't remember where she was or how she had gotten there.

Michael stood in the doorway. He was holding two brown paper bags in his hands. "I got us some food and some toothpaste and stuff."

Aileen took one of the paper bags and headed to the bathroom. Minutes later, she returned. Her wet hair was wrapped in a towel turned turban. Another towel was wrapped around her body and tucked under her arm, just above her breast.

Michael (chewing) looked up from the small kitchen table, "I….uh I wasn't sure of what you wanted so I got burgers."

While Aileen ate, Michael went to the shower. Towel drying his dark brown hair, he returned to find Aileen in bed, covered by the green bedspread.

Outside, it had begun to rain. The sound of rain drops hitting the puddles beneath the window was hypnotic.

He moved slowly to the bed, pulled the covers back and climbed into bed next to her. For the first time he felt her naked body against his. His body stiffened at the touch of her skin. And ……it rained.

He took her face gently into his hand and turned it to face his. Kissing her lips, he inhaled her breath, which reminded him of peaches, ripe peaches. Peaches so pink, so ripe and so ready that with the least bit of urging, would fall from the limbs supporting them.

Her lips so soft that he thought surely he could sink right through them. Oh…….The Rain.

Her body trembled as his hand slipped to her hips and pulled her nude body closer to his. The rain pounded the tin roof top; the sound of flowing water seemed to be everywhere. The Rain…..The Rain

The sensation was so strong, that Michael thought he could feel each drop, striking the bare skin covering his entire body. Aaah…..The Rain….

Droplets hit the sill of the open window and splashed onto their faces. Oh….The Rain. Mouth to mouth and body to body they clung to each other moving to the beating, thumping, hammering rhythm of ….The Rain…The Rain…The Rain

A burst of thunder roared up Michael's spine, down his arm and through his thigh, his body jerked and jerked again. ..The Rain….

Aileen's body now limp, quieted as bodies entwined Mr. and Mrs. Michael Crenshaw slept.

Weeks after arriving at the Travel Court, Michael and Aileen became friendly with the neighbors who lived in the cottage next to theirs. Their names were Della and James Sterling. The Sterlings, like most of the people at the court, had traveled to Oklahoma to find work. James, like many of the men at the travel court, worked on one of the government sponsored work projects. He recommended that Michael apply, which he did, and got a job working to build and repair streets.

Earning enough money to pay their expenses while in Oklahoma, Michael was careful not to spend the savings he had tucked away for emergencies and for further travel. His new plan firmly in mind and on paper, he and Aileen discussed what they would do next.

They would stay in Oklahoma until the baby was born. They would then start traveling toward Wyoming, where Michael planned to buy back the land once owned by his grandfather. He would seek out jobs to sustain them as they travel. Once in Wyoming, he would begin his horse breeding and training business.

Michael grew excited just talking about the plan, while Aileen worried about how Michael really felt about the baby and if he would ever be able to love it.

As planned, they stayed at the travel court in Oklahoma until the baby was born. Della and James, both in their mid-forties, had lived in the cottage community longer than anyone else. They were well-liked and respected in the small community of cottages. They were knowledgeable about most of what went on, who you could trust and who you should not share personal information with.

The wife, Della, helped Aileen to find a midwife. Luckily, the midwife also lived in the camp. The three women would spend their days cleaning, making meals and getting prepared for the new arrival. Della and the midwife would discuss with Aileen what to expect to happen before, during and after the delivery. But no one could tell her how to love a baby conceived in hate.

Surprisingly, the birth went smoothly, considering that Aileen, for the last nine months, had spent most mornings slumped over the commode, regurgitating whatever she had last eaten.

The women from the community of cottages came over to help with the cooking and the cleaning until Aileen was able to care for herself and the baby.

Michael had purchased a used crib at one of the local thrift stores and the ladies had brought over used baby clothes and diapers that they no longer needed.

The baby was growing and getting stronger daily. However, Aileen had developed a cough and could not seem to get rid of it. Della insisted that she see the doctor.

Aileen refused. She was sure that once she got rested, she would soon feel better. She would not waste money. Michael had been working too hard to save enough money so that they could move on with the next phase of their plan, she reasoned.

One evening Michael came home to find Quinn in his crib. It was obvious that he needed changing and had needed it for quite a while. Aileen was lying in bed, the sheets were wet, and she was barely conscious.

Grabbing Quinn, Michael ran to Della's house, banged on the door, and asked if she could watch Quinn while he took Aileen to the doctor. Handing Quinn to Della, he ran back to his cottage, wrapped Aileen in a blanket, put her in the truck and sped off toward town to the doctor's office.

The doctor said that the most important thing was to get Aileen's fever down. Her skin was burning to the touch. After a series of questions about what she had eaten, where she had been, had she been bitten by insect, the doctor said he would have to do some test. Aileen would need to be admitted to the hospital immediately, in order to run test.

For a week, after Aileen was admitted into the hospital, Michael spent every free minute at her bedside waiting for her to awaken. Aileen's body had begun to swell. The doctor said that her body was creating fluid faster than it was able to eliminate it.

After the longest seven days in Michael's life, Aileen stirred, her eyes opened and she looked over at Michael. "What happened?" she asked. "Where is the baby?"

“Quinn is with Della. You have been sick for a week. How do you feel?” asked Michael.

The doctor entered the room, followed closely by the nurse. Looking down at the chart in his hand he said, “Mrs. Crenshaw, the swelling in your feet and legs is down, and we have managed to stabilize your temperature. However, you need to know that your test shows that you have “Bright” disease.

Aileen looked at Michael. “Bright disease, what is that? What does all that mean doctor?” “Is she dying, will she get better. What?”

The doctor replied that he had no answers for Michael’s question. Bright, a disease of the kidney, affected people differently. Some patients claim to have been cured by drinking their own urine; some used herbal remedies, some people traveled to the Hot Springs of Arkansas. There was lots of research being done, but as yet, there had been no official cure announced in the medical community.

The doctor recommended a change in Aileen’s diet and said that if she felt the least bit tired, she was to lay down immediately and rest. The doctor told them about a new pain relieving medicine. It was new to the pharmaceutical market and received high marks for pain relief. Aileen was to take a pill whenever she was in pain.

Returning to their cottage that night, Aileen climbed into bed. Michael went next door to get Quinn. In his blue cotton pajamas and wrapped in a dark blue blanket, Quinn was fast asleep when Michael picked him up from Della’s sofa and headed home.

“How is she?” Della asked.

“Still a little weak, but she is getting better. Thank you for your help, Della.”

“Always,” Della responded. “I’ll be over in the morning to help out. Goodnight.”

A week later, Michael found himself sitting on the side of the bed, watching as Aileen slept with Quinn tucked in the small of her arms. Michael thought, "Do I tell her now? She is still so weak. Do I tell her about David?"

Michael had heard from some of the men on his job about the sawmill explosion. In disbelief, he had stopped at the corner store on the way home to buy a newspaper. He needed to read the article for himself. He had to be sure before he told Aileen. Clover Grove was such a small place, everybody knew everyone else. He looked at the names of the injured, he recognized them all, and then he looked at the names of the dead: David Paul Sumpner, 19 husband and father of one.

She had to know, and it had to be him who told her. "Aileen, baby, wake up there's something I have to tell you." Already weakened by the fever and infection, Aileen pulled the covers over her head and wept. Michael gently pulled Quinn from her arms, laid him in his crib, crawled into bed, and held her through the night.

As the days went by, Aileen began to regain her strength enough to clean the cottage, cook and spend time sitting in the front yard with the neighborhood women and their children.

Michael continued his work. Aileen's illness had set their plan back six months, but Michael was just glad to have her healthy again. Michael had heard from some of the men on his job that there was a movie theatre in town and thought it would be a good idea for the two of them to have a night out.

The theatre was located between the bank and Weissen Dress store downtown. There were lights surrounding a giant crown-shaped board flashing; "Showing Tonight, "Gone with the Wind." Aileen could hardly wait to get inside.

After the movie, Michael suggested that they go to the café down the street for coffee and maybe a piece of pie. Aileen agreed. They walked the block down the street, went in the café and sat at one of the booths.

Sitting at the table next to them was a rather large gentleman wearing a cowboy hat, crocodile cowboy boots, and a cowboy belt with a buckle to match the emblem embroidered on his shirt. He was flirting outrageously with all the waitresses, who seemed to be enjoying the attention.

"Hey there, fellow, that sure is a pretty little lady you've got there. I used to have a girlfriend with fire red hair. Boy did I love that lady and that fire red hair!"

Michael didn't know whether to take offense or not. The older gentlemen didn't seem to be threatening. Noticing the strained looks on Aileen and Michael's faces, one of the waitresses came over to their booth.

Between chews of the gum she had in her mouth, she said, "Oh, don't pay any attention to Charlie. Everybody here knows him, he is just a big old Teddy Bear."

Realizing that he may have offended Michael, the older gentleman asked, "Hey, can I buy you and your lady a cup of coffee?"

Aileen nudged Michael and almost together they said, "Yes".

The old gentlemen moved over to their booth and sat next to Michael. They began to talk and found out that Charlie was actually Charlie Westland of Westland Ranches. He owned several ranches, one each in the Texas hill country, Oklahoma and Colorado. He traveled among each of the ranches, stopping at particular cafes along the way. In his travels, he had come to know many of the owners and staff of these establishments.

Michael told him about his work and his plan to one day own a ranch, where he would breed show horses. Charlie thought this was a great plan and was impressed by Michael's drive and ability to set up and follow his plan. Having made his money in cattle, he said he had himself been considering venturing into show horses.

Michael and Charlie agreed that in a month Michael and Aileen would join him at his Colorado ranch to start plans for the Show horse breeding venture.

Chapter 14

Colorado landscape was different from anything Michael and Aileen had ever seen. The great mountains of different colors some matte and some brilliant, seem to shoot up from the ground. From the road, they could see snow on the mountain tops in the distance.

According to Charlie's directions, they were to drive about 20 miles west of the city of Colorado Springs. Colorado Springs was a beautiful city, which sat at the base of Pikes Peak.

Because of its domed shape, beautiful red color, and height of over 14,000 feet above sea level, Pikes Peak had become a popular tourist attraction. Colorado Springs, which had been established in the early 1800's as a supply town for those who mined for minerals at Pikes Peak, had become a tourist attraction as well.

Aileen begged Michael to stop for a bit so that they could get out and walk around the city. She was mesmerized as they walked from one shop to the next. Tribesmen were selling pottery, blankets, rugs, baskets and jewelry from wagons parked alongside the street. Aileen was fully captivated by the new experience. She was fascinated by the people who looked so much alike but claimed, by the signs on their merchandise, to be from the Hopi, Navajo or Pueblo tribe.

Aileen tried on a silver ring with a turquoise stone. Michael conceded and purchased it for her. They left the merchants having purchased a handwoven poncho for Michael and buckskin moccasins with green, blue and red beads at the toe for Quinn.

As they were about to get back in the truck, there was a roaring noise overhead; other people seem to ignore it. Michael and Aileen wondered if only they had heard the rumbling loud noise. They both looked to the sky to see an airplane overhead.

Michael shouted, "Look Aileen it's an aero plane!" Neither of the two of them had ever seen one before. Quinn, in Michael's arms, began to cry, disturbed from his sleep by the incredible noise.

It was dark when they finally reached the mammoth gate attached to woven wire fencing. The large metal letters overhead announced "Westland Ranch". Michael got out of the truck, opened the gate, and drove down the dark road to the massive plantation styled house. It seemed Charlie was waiting up for them. In every window across the front of the house was light.

Michael got out of the car and approached the house. A barking sound came from the porch. Two porch lanterns attached to the walls on either side of the massive double door, flashed on. Through the door, stepped Charlie, smiling.

"Glad to see you, boy," he said, reaching out to shake Michael's hand. "Where is the rest of the family?" he asked looking around and behind Michael.

"In the truck," Michael answered," waving to Aileen to join them on the porch. Aileen, carrying the sleeping Quinn, opened the truck door and joined the two men on the long and wide covered porch.

"Come in, come in," Charlie said, opening the door further and stepping back inside to allow Aileen and her bundle to pass. As she entered what was the most magnificent room she had ever seen, she thought, "Surely this room is twice the size of the auditorium at John Logan Bryant High School." Aileen tried not to stare, but stood in amazement looking at the giant five tier crystal and gold chandelier that hung in the center of the room.

The room was filled with beautiful furniture, masculine and yet extraordinarily elegant. A beautiful dark brown leather sofa was placed in front of the massive fireplace, in which four average size men could comfortably stand. Over the fireplace was a gigantic vibrant painting of the Rosslyn, a historic English chapel. In the center of the floor, a large oriental rug was flanked on either side by two settees covered in cowhide.

"You two have got to be hungry," Charlie said," and the baby must be hungry as well."

Quinn started to stir and wanted to be released from Aileen's arm. Holding on to his hand, she gently stooped to stand him on the beautiful, dark wood, paneled floor. "I guess we could use a sandwich," she replied.

"Good," Charlie said, pressing the bell on the side of the wall. "I'll have Margarit to make sandwiches.

A very attractive young woman entered the room, dressed in a black knee length dress, topped by a white bibbed apron, which was tied in back. Her long straight black hair secured in a bun in back of her head. "Did you want something, Mr. Westland?" She asked."

"Yes, sandwiches for my guests please, Margarit. And something to drink, what would you like?"

"Iced tea, if you have it. I would love some iced tea."

The meal only served to make Aileen sleepier, and Charlie could see that her eyes were growing heavy. "Margarit, come and show Mrs. Crenshaw to their room. Michael and I have a little business planning to discuss before we retire."

Michael went to the car and gathered their bags and followed Margarit as she led them up the long curving stairs. She opened the door to their room. After over a year of living in a small one-room cottage, to Aileen and Michael, this seemed like paradise.

The bed, covered in a silk bedspread and stack of decorative pillows, had to be big enough to sleep four adults, thought Aileen, pulling back the covers to lay Quinn down.

"Do you need anything more?" Margarit asked." There is a bathroom down the hall, the second door on the left."

"No, thank you," Aileen replied, as she hurriedly undressed and put on her night gown. "The bath will have to wait until tomorrow," she thought as she climbed into the giant silky covered bed next to Quinn.

Downstairs Michael and Charlie were plotting out plans for tomorrow. Charlie was aware of a farmer about 10 miles east, who had come into possession of two thoroughbreds that he was interested in selling.

Charlie thought he and Michael might drive down first thing in the morning to look them over.

Aileen arose to find Michael's side of the bed wrinkled and empty. Walking across the thick olive green rug to the windows, which stretched from floor to ceiling, she pulled back the long silky fabric of the drapes to look out at the landscape of the ranch. "How can stone have so many beautiful colors, brilliant reds, yellows, greys, browns, even pinks? The storm that created these splendid structures must have been colossal." she thought. A scuffling noise interrupted her thoughts causing her to look behind her. Quinn was standing beside the bed rubbing his eyes. "Are you hungry?" she asked.

Quinn nodded yes.

"Then let's get bathed and go downstairs to see what there is to eat."

At the stove, Margarit was busy forcing a large piece of crockery into the oven.

“Good morning, Margarit, this is my son, Quinn. We thought we would see what there is for breakfast.”

“Good morning, Mrs. Crenshaw.” Aileen was a little stunned, though Margarit looked Spanish there was absolutely no trace of an accent when she spoke.

Margarit served breakfast at the smaller table in the kitchen. Invited by Aileen, she sat to join Aileen and Quinn for bacon, eggs, sausage, grits, biscuits and syrup. Margarit explained that Charlie, Michael and her husband, Miguel had gone to look at horses about ten miles away.

The two women talked as Margarit cleared the table and washed the dishes. They found that they were similar in lots of ways. Though she was four years older than Aileen, Margarit had no children. She and her husband lived in one of the many smaller houses on the ranch. She too loved to knit, garden and cook.

Curiously, Aileen asked about Margarit’s accent. Margarit explained that she had attended Catholic Schools in New York City, which was her birthplace. She and her husband had returned to the Colorado area, where his family was from, once the Depression had grown serious and it became impossible to find work.

Just before sundown and just in time for dinner, the men returned. They were in good spirits as they talked about the deal they had made for the thoroughbreds.

“Time to wash up for dinner.’ Aileen said. “Go with your father, Quinn, and get washed up.”

"Daddy, Daddy," Quinn screamed, running to Michael who scooped him up into his arms. Quinn and Michael ascended the stairs.

At the dinner table, the men discussed the events of the day: the seller, a small farm owner, had inherited two thoroughbreds for which he had no use. The farmer's brother owned a farm severely damaged by the Dust Storm in the most southeastern part of Colorado and had given the horses over to his brother. The brother put them up for sale, since he could no longer afford their upkeep.

Charlie took pleasure in explaining how Michael had done the figures and had shown the farmer that it was better to sell the two horses for 500 dollars each instead of the $750 each he had at first requested. Factoring in the cost to feed the horses and stabling them, the farmer had agreed and made a deal to sell them both for $1000.

Aileen took Quinn up to bed, and the two men stayed down to plan out their next coup.

Early the next morning, Aileen and Quinn were sitting on the veranda, watching the daily activities of the ranch, when they spotted a large blue car, followed by a cloud of dust speeding toward the house. The car pulled to stop just inches before hitting the steps.

Out of the car stepped a somewhat handsome man, of about thirty. His dark hair kept falling into his red bloodshot eyes.

"Heck of a ride, aint it honey?" he said to no one in particular, dusting the gray Stetson hat he held in his hands against his pant leg.

Aileen was caught off guard by the stranger's behavior, but she was almost positive that he was drunk.

"If you are looking for Charlie, he is in the fields with the horses." she offered.

Naw, I'll see him when he gets in," he responded pushing the door open and entering the house. Throwing his hat over onto the brown leather sofa, he proceeded to go upstairs.

Aileen grabbed Quinn's hand and rushed to the kitchen. Margarit was busy plucking the feathers from a chicken, in preparation for the night's dinner.

"There is a man upstairs, he just walked in the door and went upstairs."

Margarit left her chore for a minute and went to look outside at the long blue car, carelessly parked in the front yard. When she returned to the kitchen she said, "That's Jake, Mr. Charlie's nephew, Jake. Be careful around him. He tends to drink too much, and he can get nasty when he is drunk. He's not much better when he is sober either."

Aileen sat at the table, and Margarit told her about Mr. Charlie's only sister, who had died when Jake was a teenager, how Charlie had promised to take care of Jake, the result of which was a spoiled, useless, over-indulged man. Jake only stopped by once every four to five months, usually broke and in need of funds for some great venture he had in the making.

That evening, Charlie and Michael came in hungry as usual. Each man went to his separate baths to get cleaned up for dinner. They returned and joined Aileen and Quinn at the custom-made mahogany dining room table inlaid with banded tiger wood.

"There is a nasty man here." Quinn said.

Aileen's mouth dropped, she had not remembered to caution Quinn not to discuss today's conversation. "I believe your nephew, Jake, is here," she stated.

"Jake! Well where is that scoundrel?" Charlie asked in his thunderous baritone.

Hearing the question, Jake appeared at the top of the stairs. "Here I am Uncle C," he said, sliding down the rails of the staircase. He joined everyone else at the dinner table.

Margarit came in with a platter, piled high with golden brown, baked chicken. As if being guided by past experience, she cautiously passed Jake's chair. Jake looked up at her and seemed to leer. Aileen wondered if anyone else had seen this, or if, stimulated by the earlier conversation, her imagination was working in over drive.

After dinner, Aileen, holding Quinn's protesting hand went upstairs to bed. The men remained downstairs discussing the day's events and plans. After a glass of brandy each, Michael said his goodnights and went upstairs to join Aileen and Quinn.

Jake lifted the crystal decanter, poured the brown liquid into snifters for both himself and Charlie. Sinking into one of the large brown leather Chippendale chairs, he began to pitch his new business proposal and the cost to initiate it.

Jake explained that he and a group of investors were going to build and open a new casino in Las Vegas. If Charlie could front him the initial investment of $100,000, he was sure the business would be a success. Las Vegas, he said, was booming. It was the gambling capital of the world and ready for more casinos.

Sipping from his glass, Charlie listened to Jake's proposal. Careful not to mention any of the previous failed schemes that Jake had undertaken at his expense, he tells Jake that he himself has taken on a new venture in breeding show horses.

With a degree of optimistic pride, Charlie states that he has so far invested $ 150,000 into a very promising horse breeding business. He has already purchased 10 thoroughbreds and has plans to buy more, once the four that are ready to show, are sold at the big show in Pennsylvania.

He will loan Jake $10,000 but nothing more. And this will be the last venture that he will sponsor. Charlie has never said the word “last” to Jake before; this is new terminology. In spite of the constant warning about being more frugal and growing up, Charlie has never refused to give him money.

Jake lifted his glass and gulped down the last of his brandy. He poured another and gulped that one as well. He then slammed his glass down on the antique, marble top table.

He looked at Charlie with a vengeance that had never existed between the two men and walked out. Charlie turned off the parlor lights, climbed the winding stairs and went to bed as well.

As usual, the men are already gone when Aileen awakened. Grabbing her robe, she walked over pulled back the drapes and looked out of the window. Glancing back at Quinn quietly sleeping, she thought, “What a beautiful place to raise a child.”

She decided to hurry downstairs to get towels for the morning baths and get back before Quinn awakened.

As she entered the kitchen, she could hear scuffling. She heard a woman’s voice crying… yelling “No….No….. Get off of me……Get off of me!”

Aileen pushed through the kitchen door to see Margarit on the floor, legs spread apart, and dress pull above her waist, her long, black hair scattered about her head.

Food from the earlier breakfast was scattered over the floor. The large wooden bowl Margarit used to prepare bread was turned over just above her head. Various utensils were strewn over the table.

Jake was lying on top of her, trying with one hand to hold her down and with the other to get his pajama pants open. Margarit was using her free hand to push and claw at Jakes chest and face. She was attempting to twist her body in an effort to flip Jake off of her.

Aileen looked over to the stove and spotted a large iron frying skillet. She grabbed the skillet with both hands and swung it with every bit of strength that she could muster. With the rage of four years of haunted sleep, she lifted the iron skillet again and again and again.

Tears streamed down her face as she remembered hands over her mouth. She hammered the skillet against Jake's head, his back, and his buttocks. Jake lifted his hands and cried, "Help me! Stop, please! Somebody help me!"

Aileen slammed the skillet against his hands. Remembering the touch of unwanted hands pulling at her clothing, her legs, her breast, she swung with uncontrolled fury. Over and over again, she swung the iron pan. She was lost in a state of madness.

Suddenly, she felt someone pulling her away. Someone's hands were around her waist and pulling as hard as they could to get her away from Jake.

"Miss Aileen, Miss Aileen, you'll kill him! Stop before you kill him!"

Jake was lying on the floor, his knees pulled up to his chest, in a fetal position, sobbing.

"Get out of here before my husband does kill you, you disgusting maggot!" Margarit shouted.

Looking down at the bloody mess that was Jake, the two women make an unspoken vow that for the protection of their husbands and Charlie, this was an incident that never occurred.

As the two women went about cleaning the bloody floor, Margarit tearfully confides in Aileen that this was not the first time that she has been attacked by Jake. She thanks Aileen for helping her. "Jake, Margarit exclaims, is an evil evil man."

At dinner that evening, Charlie was not surprised that Jake was gone. It is so typical of him to blow in one minute with some wild dream and be gone the next minute.

At breakfast the next morning, Michael walked into the dining room to find Charlie looking down at the table. His intense thoughts showed on his face. Michael said, "Hey old man, a penny for your thoughts."

Charlie had not seen Michael come in. He looked up and said, "I wouldn't want to cheat you out of your penny, son." They both laughed.

Charlie told Michael that he had been out in the stable and noticed that one of his most valuable saddles was missing. He was sure that Jake had taken it. The inability to take responsibility for himself was a character flaw that Jake had had all of his life.

Michael agreed to drive with Charlie to Colorado Springs that evening. According to Charlie, Jake usually took the things he stole to the pawn shops in Colorado Springs. At Gill's Pawn Shop on 3rd

Street, displayed prominently in the window, was Charlie's $12,000 antique hand stitched saddle, labeled great deal $2,500.

After seeing the receipt of ownership produced by Charlie, the proprietor was willing to give back the saddle for the $800 he had given Jake for the saddle.

"You know, people are saying that Jake is in trouble with some really bad people up in Las Vegas," the proprietor offered, "They say he owes the casino almost $100,000. I don't know how he got in that deep. But if you see him, tell him people are looking for him."

Chapter 15

Michael had telephoned to say that things had gone well at the Devon Horse Show in Philadelphia. Three of the four thoroughbreds that they had taken had actually sold for twice what they had expected, and the other had sold for just under what they had predicted.

Michael said that they had also gained clients, who wanted them to train their horses for racing competitions. So Charlie was thinking of expanding the business to include race horses. If all goes well and they run into no bad weather, they should be home on Saturday.

Yelping sounds coming from the north edge of the wire fence caught Aileen's attention. She looked to see a mother coyote watching her three pups playing in the dusty red dirt aside the road. Aileen, sitting in one of the large white metal chairs on the plank-floored veranda, watched the brownish, gray fur-covered group, the mother's white-tipped, pointed ears, ever alert for signs of danger. Aileen thought, 'Mothers.'

Quinn, chasing tumble weeds across the yard, had stopped to look also. Aileen thought, "It's hard to believe that it's been two years since we came to Colorado." Quinn, who has grown to a handsome three year old would soon be four. She thought, "It's time to plan his birthday party."

Hearing the familiar clanking of bouncing metal banging against metal, Quinn recognized the sound of Charlie's big truck, pulling the empty horse trailer over the bumpy dirt road. Quinn ran to the dirt road to meet the truck. "Daddy!" he yelled.

Michael and Charlie, wearing day old beards and head-to-toe road dust, entered the room to find Aileen, Miguel and Margarit standing around the dining room table. A blue birthday cake trimmed with white icing, with the word 'Quinn' in the center sat on the table.

"It's my birthday!" Quinn shrieked. "Daddy, did you get me a present?"

"What about this?" Michael said. He reached inside the box he was holding and displayed a wooden, hand-craved, brown and white thoroughbred horse.

Quinn's green eyes lit up, as he grabbed the horse and ran through the house making horse sounds.

"Cake", Aileen offers.

"Later maybe, now I need to get a good bath and shave." said Michael.

Charlie nodded in agreement, and both men went their separate ways to get cleaned up.

That night after dinner, Michael came upstairs to join Aileen and Quinn. Quinn was kneeling in front of the bed, playing with his toy horse.

"Aileen, you know we have done really well here. In another six months, we will have enough money to make a substantial down payment on the property in Wyoming. And Charlie has promised to let me buy two of the breed mares that he bought last month. I guess, what I'm trying to say is, it may be time to start thinking about leaving," Michael said.

Aileen, who was lying on the custom made French brocade sofa, which spans the length of one wall, looked up but did not respond.

The words did not come easy to Aileen. Though she knew that one day they would need to move on, the thought of uprooting Quinn again brought about mixed feeling. She loved the adventuresome side of Michael, willing to try new things, sometimes acting at the spur of the moment and yet keeping a steady eye on his plan.

"Have you talked to Charlie?" Aileen asked.

"Not yet, Michael said, walking over to kiss Aileen on her forehead. He sat at the other end of the sofa, lifted her feet and put them in his lap.

"He has always known about our plans for Wyoming. I will talk to him sometime this week," he said, rubbing Aileen's feet.

"Mmmm, that feels good, Mr. Crenshaw." Aileen said.

"Just wait until our son is asleep," Michael whispered.

"Promises," Aileen retorted.

Aileen awoke to find Michael gone as usual. "Promises," she smiled to herself, thinking about Michael and how as soon as his head hit the pillow he was fast asleep. "Promises," she thought.

Leaving Quinn asleep, she showered, dressed and headed downstairs. As she started down the stairs, she could see Michael sitting in one of the large brown leather Chippendale chairs, reading the newspaper.

"Why are you still here?" She asked, "Where is Charlie?"

"He was gone when I came downstairs. Margarit said there had been an urgent telephone call, something to do with Jake, so Charlie has gone to Las Vegas. I thought I would wait and have breakfast with you and Quinn, since we never get to share breakfast. What do you think?"

"I think that's a great idea. Let me get Quinn. What did Margarit cook?"

Aileen led Quinn who was rubbing his eyes, downstairs and into the kitchen, "Look who is having breakfast with us this morning," she said to Quinn, who beamed. "Daddy!"

After breakfast, Michael left Aileen and Quinn in the kitchen and headed for the barn and the horses.

Two days passed and there was no word from Charlie, then a week passed. Michael was growing increasingly worried.

He asked Aileen, "Do you think we need to call the police?"

"Did he leave a number where he could be reached? Margarit, Margarit, did Charlie leave a number. Did he say where he would be staying?"

"Hello, can you get me the police?" Michael said to the operator.

The sheriff arrived to take a missing person's report. Sheriff Tate, a tall man with hints of silver at the temples of his light brown hair, and a little too much expanse in his waist line, told Michael that they will be contacting the Las Vegas police department.

Sheriff Tate, well-known throughout the county, had held the title of sheriff for the past 20 years. He would ask the Las Vegas police to check for any record of Charlie at any hotels or hospitals in the area. Meanwhile, he would have his deputies check all the local hospitals, hotels, gas stations and other local establishments.

The entire night, Michael paced the dark, mahogany-wood floors. The wrenching, churning feeling in his stomach would not allow him to settle in one spot. For the first time in over four years, Michael considered, "could this be how our parents felt when Aileen and I disappeared?"

The next morning, well before sunlight, Michael and Miguel along with some of the farm hands got into one of the company trucks and headed out, driving the highways that Charlie would have been traveling to Las Vegas.

Less than ten miles away from the ranch, one of the hands noticed skid marks. It appeared that an automobile had swerved to miss something in the road and run off the road just before the bridge into a small lake.

The men jumped from the truck and began to run toward the tire tracks, which lead into tall bushes. Pushing through the tall brush with their bare hands, the men ran and then crawled through the muck to where they could finally see the back of Charlie's white pickup truck. The specialty license plate was visible in the moonlight. The entire front of the truck was submerged in the thick, black, murky water.

Michael screamed, "Charlie, Charlie!" the other men joined in the call, "Mr. Charlie, Mr. Charlie" hoping upon hope that Charlie had somehow managed to get out of the truck and crawl away.

Michael followed by Miguel, jumped into the water but was unable to swim or even walk in the thick mud. Backing out of the thick muck, Michael gave the keys to Miguel, "Go get help! Hurry, Hurry!"

Miguel left and was back in thirty minutes with the sheriff, an ambulance and a tow truck.

"We will have to wait until we can get the truck out. There is no way to tell if he is still inside until we lift that truck out. I'm sorry, Michael but that's the only way," explained Sheriff Tate. " It's just too dangerous to work out here right now. We have to wait until daylight.

Michael, Miguel and the farm hands returned to their truck parked by the side of the road and sat, waiting for sunlight, so that Charlie's truck could be pulled from the murky waters.

Standing outside the driver's side door, Sheriff Tate consoled, "Sorry, Michael, its Charlie. He's inside, he's gone."

"No," Michael lips released a dry moan, putting his head on the steering wheel as the tears fell into his lap. The men in the truck cried. For the loss of a friend, they cried.

Aileen looked up to see Michael and Miguel walking through the door. The expression on their faces was all she needed to answer the unspoken question. "Gone?" she said.

Michael slumped to a chair at the foyer table, looked down at the floor, and nodded, "yes."

So many questions flooded Aileen's mind, but for now, she thought, I will let the men have their time. She left Michael and Miguel inside and went to sit on the veranda with Quinn and Margarit.

Two days after Charlie's body had been found, Jake arrived with his attorney in tow. As the only heir to the property, he wanted to get the property back in working order, which meant he wanted all the leeches off the property now. He expounded. He wanted the property cleared immediately.

The same day that Jake arrived, Miguel and Margarit packed and vacated the property.

Michael explained that it would take a few days for him to gather all their things and be off the property. To this response, Jake called the Sheriff's office. Sheriff Tate arrived and explained to Jake that until the will was read, he had no right to evict anyone.

Immediately after the funeral, Charlie's attorney came over to the ranch with Charlie's will. Aileen and Michael were busy upstairs packing. There was a gentle tapping at the door. Aileen crossed the floor to the door and opened it.

"Excuse me, Miss, my name is Aaron Bergstein, I am....was Charlie Westland's attorney. Would you and your husband please join us in the parlor?"

At Mr. Bergstein's suggestion, the meeting was moved to the dining table for more seating.

Seated at the table, Aaron Bergstein peered over the small round framed spectacles, which hung at the tip of his nose. He started to read the will aloud. According to Charlie Westland's last will and testament, all his property in Texas was to be sold and the money distributed to the many friends he had made and come to love through his business travels from ranch to ranch. (Each waitress, waiter, cook, cleaner and owner was listed by name, and the nickname that Charlie had fondly given them.)

The ranch property in Oklahoma was to be sold and distributed to various named charities throughout the Colorado Springs area, which he had loved as his home.

The Colorado ranch was left to his business partner and good friend, Michael Crenshaw and his wife, Aileen.

At this, Jake shot to his feet. “This cannot be so, this is impossible. This will is forged, I’m sure of it!”

Aaron Bergstein looked up at Jake, with the practiced look of an attorney who has seen this reaction many times, and stated, “I have been Charlie Westland’s attorney for over thirty years and I can assure you that there is nothing forged or illegal about this will.”

Jake screamed, “There is no way that my uncle would leave me with nothing! No way!”

Aaron calmly looked down at the will, “You’re right, he left you $10,000 to start a venture in Las Vegas, a casino, it says here. Is that right, a casino?”

Jake slammed his fist on the table, stood and turned to leave. Hearing the commotion coming from the dining room, Quinn curiously entered the door. Jake shoved Quinn out of the doorway. Quinn fell to the floor, stunned.

Michael leaped across the table, knocking chairs, glasses and papers onto the floor. Before anyone could protest, Michael had grabbed Jake by this throat, and had him pressed against the wall. Jakes eyes had begun to bulge out of his head; he was gasping for breath. His knees were beginning to weaken; it seemed he would fall at any minute. Trying to pry Michael’s fingers from Jakes neck, Aaron and Aileen pulled as hard as they could.

“Daddeeeeeeeeee!” squealed Quinn.

Being awakened from the trance, Michael looked down to see Quinn, looking up at him in horror. He released Jake, stepped back, and sat in a chair at the dining table. Quinn crawled into his lap saying, “It’s okay, Daddy, its okay.”

Chapter 16

"A severed brake line. Are you sure, Sheriff?" Michael queried. "But how?"

Sheriff Tate had stopped by the ranch to update Michael on the investigation into Charlie's death. From the beginning, the very night that Charlie's body had been found, Sheriff Tate had had his suspicions.

Crime scene investigators discovered skid marks from a second automobile and were searching for automobiles with tires that would match. There had been too many unanswered questions.

Why had Jake not filed a missing person report? Why had Jake not been concerned that no one had heard from Charlie in over a week? What was the urgent event that Charlie was rushing to? These were all questions the sheriff had posed to Jake. Needless to say, Jake had no satisfactory answers and had referred the Sheriff to his attorney for any further questions.

The case, Sheriff Tate said, would remain open and under further investigation, until they had developed enough evidence to take to the district attorney.

Aileen had located Margarit and Miguel and convinced them to return to work at the ranch.

Aileen offered Margarit and Miguel one of the three guest suites in the manor house, but Margarit assured them that she and Miguel would be much more comfortable in the smaller house they had shared before.

Aileen and Margarit went on about the business of maintaining the house, while Michael and Miguel took care of the business of the horses. The business had picked up substantially. With the addition of training race horses, Michael had to hire additional help. Delivering and showing horses meant that Michael had to travel all over the country, and he had begun to travel to England and Spain.

Aileen spent most of her time in one of the several gardens around the house. She planted whatever the dry, hot, climate of Colorado would allow. In spite of the climate, she was able to develop relatively robust vegetable, herb and flower gardens.

At four years old, Quinn was a bright and energetic boy. Aileen had already started his home schooling. A fast learner, he had almost completed his first grade reader. Whenever he would come to the kitchen to help out, Margarit would teach him Spanish words. So at four years old, Quinn was almost fluent in Spanish, a feat that neither Aileen nor Michael could claim.

Lately Aileen had found herself tiring easily. She thought "it's just the heat." Medically speaking, she had been doing very well, since that bout in Oklahoma. She had not been sick the entire time that they had been in Colorado. She had begun thinking maybe all she needed, after all, was a change in climate.

But as the days and weeks went on, she was fighting to stay on her feet, and the pain had returned. She was finding it difficult to hold on to her gardening tools. Her hands and feet were beginning to swell. She would have to go to Colorado Springs to see the doctor.

Michael was traveling and would not be back for a week, she told Margarit. Margarit agreed to drive with her to Colorado Springs to the doctors.

Dr. Jill Rathannis was a specialist in internal medicine. A tiny blond of about forty years old, with steel grey eyes, she had been recommended by Aileen and Michael's family doctor. According to the information given to Aileen in the field of internal medicine, Dr. Rathannis was the best.

Dr. Rathannis explained that she would need to do some tests, and for the tests, Aileen would have to spend at least one night in the hospital.

Aileen and Margarit agreed that Margarit would return to the ranch and stay with Quinn. Aileen made Margarit promise not to tell Michael that she was ill. Margarit would return the next day to pick up Aileen for the drive home.

It was a week before Dr. Rathannis called. Aileen's kidney condition was getting worse. She could continue her daily activity, but she would continue to get weaker. There were some promising new experimental drug treatments being done in the eastern part of the country.

Aileen, distraught, made a decision. She wanted to go home to see her Mama.

"No one said anything about my dying," Aileen reassured Michael. "Dr. Rathannis said that my test showed a slight weakening of my kidneys. She did not say start digging a grave."

"I feel fine, just like everyone else, some days are better than others. Michael, it has been a long time since we were home. Quinn is almost six years old, I think it's time for him to meet his family." Aileen explained.

Reluctantly Michael agreed. “You know I won’t be able to travel with you two. There is just too much to do here, and I will be traveling again in less than a month.”

Aileen agreed and assured Michael that she and Quinn would be fine. “What do you want me to tell your parents?”

“Tell my mom and Carol that I love them and will see them as soon as I can get away for any extended time.”

“And, your Dad?”

Michael did not answer, instead walked over to kiss her on the forehead, and then walked out the door.

Chapter 17

Lying on a patchwork quilt, under the big oak tree next to the pond, Aileen felt, “It’s so good to be home, back in my most favorite place on earth.”

On the hill, she could see Quinn and Lilla chasing the hens up and down the clover-covered hill. “He seems so happy here with his cousin and his young aunts,” she thought.

Lying back against the tree, she could feel the cool breeze cross her face. She closed her eyes to listen to the wind. The feel of something on her cheek startled her, and she opened her eyes to see Quinn and Lilla handing her wildflowers. “Here, Mommy, these are for you.”

“Thank you, my darlings,” she responded and lifted to give them both a kiss. They smiled and ran off to find new adventures.

In the distance, she could see her dad’s car shed, where he was busy working on any number of projects at the same time: Mr. McClinton’s red truck, Mr. Joseph’s old yellow tractor, and many others parked one behind the other. And somehow, he always managed to get the job done right, and on time.

This was his slogan, “Get it done right and on time.” This slogan and its practice had served Corbin Sumpner very well. Some families in the Grove had suffered terribly during the Depression. With contracts to repair machinery for the University, he had been able to provide food, shelter and clothing for his family.

Aileen beamed when she thought of her dad. Every girl thinks that her dad is handsome, but Corbin was handsome. At over 6 feet tall, the physical activity involved in removing and installing mechanical parts had enabled Corbin to maintain his muscular physique. His stark, straight hair, so black that caught by the sunlight, it sometimes looked blue, grew mulishly long, rendering him to Ella's barber chair at least once a week. The red undertone of his skin gave him a constant look of a perfect tan.

"Indeed," she thought, "mom had married a handsome man."

Giggles coming from the hill drew her attention. Running over the hill toward her were her youngest sisters, Dana, Lorraine and Grace, pushing each other back and forward, trying to see who could get to where she was lying first.

"Here, you got a letter from Michael," Dana said, handing the envelope to Aileen.

Aileen anxiously tore at the envelope and began to read the letter in silence.

"Does it say when he is coming?" Grace asked.

"No, he is still in Spain. There is some grand show there and he says he will be there, for the rest of the month." She sighed.

"Mom said it's time for supper anyway," added Grace, the youngest of the three.

Aileen picked up her quilt and folded it; the three headed up the hill. Met by Quinn and Lilla at the top of the hill, the six of them headed home.

Ella was bending to take biscuits from the oven, as they entered the back door.

“Prefect target,” twelve year old Lorraine conspired referring to the slingshot she had in her pocket.

“You wouldn’t dare!” said Dana.

“Not if you want to live to see tomorrow!” replied Ella as if she was able to read her daughters’ minds. “And you three wash your hands and set the table.”

“What can I do to help, Mom?” asked Aileen.

Ella assured Aileen that all the food was ready. Aileen looked down at Quinn and Lilla covered in dirt and grass stains. She gathered the two little one and went off to get them washed up for dinner.

At the dinner table, Amy, excited about her applications to University was full of conversation about what the counselor had said of her potential. She had maintained an overall A- average. She had been in both the school choir and band since 8th grade and the choir teacher thought she had a chance at a music scholarship. They would both be writing letters of referral in her favor to the University.

“Where is Anna?” asked Ella “She only worked until 6 tonight. I thought she would be home by now.”

Amy looked down at the silver-banded plate in front of her and mumbled, “I don’t know. Guess she had to work a little late.”

“What’s that, the third time this week?” asked Corbin.

Amy gave Lorraine and Dana a “keep your mouth shut stare.” And both lowered their heads and continued to eat.

Mixed in the conversations of the day's events, Dana found a way to work in the letter from Michael.

"Aileen said Michael is not coming; he is in Spain." Aileen looked shocked at the sudden insert of this sentence into the conversation.

"Well, I did get a letter, and Michael said he will not make it this month as he thought he would. The business has really picked up and until he can get someone trained to negotiate sales, he has to travel a lot more."

"That's the kind of life I want, full of adventure," chimed in Carlton. "I want to travel all over the world. I am going to see the Great Wall of China, the Taj Mahal in India, and the Great Pyramids in Egypt, where the God…ah.. Kings are buried, and in Africa, there are elephants as big as this house."

Hearing about the elephant as big as the house brought immediate and uncontrollable laughter from Quinn and Lilla.

"As big as the room, maybe Uncle Carlton, but I don't think they get as big as the house," Quinn offered. "At the zoo in Colorado Springs, we saw an elephant that could fit in this room. He was a giant gray and….."

"Anyway my plan is to get as far away from Clover Grove as I can. As soon as I'm old enough, I will be joining the army the very day that I turn 18. Then I'll travel all over the world."

Ella looks over at Carlton, so much like his father, the reddish undertone of his skin, deep dark black hair so straight that it seemed to spike at its ends. "Tall, handsome, and willful, just like his father," she thought.

"I'd say that's a conversation for another time," Ella said, with Corbin nodding in agreement.

After dinner, Ella and Corbin retreated to the parlor. Ella went to her nightly knitting and Corbin, his bible reading. "You know, Corbin, sooner or later we will have to address Carlton's plan of joining the military."

"He is not going to go and get himself killed. Have you forgotten all the men we lost in the last war, the Great War they called it. What is so great about war, I ask? Over one hundred thousand men died and for what?"

"I understand how you feel, Dear, but soon he will be old enough to make the decision for himself."

"Well, until that time comes, he will not be leaving to join any army, and that is final. He needs to be more focused on getting his education. He could use more time in his books." Corbin stopped to breathe in and then, "No way, Ella, there is no way a son of mine is going to go off and get himself killed."

Ella, sensing that perhaps as stated previously, this was a conversation best left to another time, simply replied, "Yes, Dear."

"He should be more like his brother, Hugh. Hugh has plans of going off to the University to study chemical engineering. Hugh and that little Guttenberg girl spend most of their free time at the high school in the lab. Carlton should find a study partner like that little Avon to help him with his studies, instead of concentrating on this fascination he has with the military."

"Yes Dear, but Carlton and Hugh are different people. Hugh has natural talents that Carlton does not have. Hugh has always been good with his books. That comes easy to him. Carlton has always had to struggle with mathematics and reading, not to speak of science. So don't be so hard on him. I'm sure he is doing his best." Ella defended.

Ella, attempting to change the subject, said, "You know dear, I think it's time to add the room that we had talked about. Claudia has been dating a man who is supposed to be a good builder. He did some work on the church and the building committee was greatly pleased with it."

"This weekend, when Claudia comes to spend time with Lilla, I will ask her about him. Ben Owens, I think that's his name."

"Who....?" Corbin asked, still trapped in the previous conversation.

"Claudia, Lilla's grandmother. She is here every weekend, have you forgotten Claudia? Getting old, old man."

Lorraine, Dana and Grace were busy getting ready for bed and school the next morning. Amy and Aileen were cleaning the kitchen, when there was a tapping at the kitchen window. Aileen pulled back the curtains and looked out to see Anna.

"Open the door," Anna mouthed.

"Where have you been?" Aileen asked, turning the lock on the door.

"Don't even ask," sniped Amy. "She has a secret lover."

"Do I smell alcohol on your breath, Anna? Have you been drinking?"

Anna pushed pass Aileen and went to the girls' bedroom.

"He's married," Amy said, as Anna left the room.

"A married man?" Aileen said stunned. "But who, who is he?"

"I don't know; she won't say."

The nightmare had been so real that it caused Corbin to wake up shaking and drenched in sweat. It had been years since he had had to deal with these dreams:

Engulfed by thick black smoke, he found it difficult, almost impossible to breath, causing him to cough uncontrollably. In the distance, he could hear the screaming of others, searching for loss family members. He could see forms moving around him but no faces.

He covered his nose and mouth with his hand in an attempt to ward off the overwhelming stench of the dead and dying. The ground was littered with twisted and mangled flesh. Men moaned from open wounds, and missing limbs. He did not know where, but he knew that his brother was lying among the dead and dying in this cold, dark, isolate place.

He heard his brother's voice as clear as day. "Corbin! Corbin! Help me, help me please! Come and get me I want to come home!

Torn and burned flesh covers the ground. Men with missing and torn limbs trudged about, looking for their missing body parts. So vivid, so real, is the dream that Corbin can smell the blood. Blood, so thick, that he can taste it. He sees himself walking among the bloody bodies, searching for his brother. He can hear his brother's voice, pleading in the distance.

"Corbin, I want to go home!" But Corbin cannot find his brother.

He can feel the thick red squishing mass between his toes. The blood is getting thicker and flows like a slow oozing river.

"Corbin, I want to come home!"

With each step, Corbin sinks deeper and deeper. The blood covers his shoes and travels up his legs and still he cannot find his brother.

Corbin spots his brother, his twisted body, lying at the base of a giant old willow tree, his arms stretched out reaching for him. His body covered in blood, he cries out for help. Corbin stretches out his arm and reaches for his brother. He can almost touch his fingertips.

And then always at this point, the dream abruptly ends.

Corbin crawled out of bed as not to awaken Ella, and walked toward the kitchen for a glass of water.

Standing in front of the cupboard, he remembers the day that he and his younger brother had decided to enlist, to do their part for the country. His brother was accepted. He had been denied. An accident of his youth had left Corbin with a slight limp on his right side. A wagon had turned over atop of him, breaking his ankle. The doctor had done such a crude job of resetting his bone that it left him with a slight limp.

He remembered the last time he saw his brother at the train station, waving good bye. So proud was he, to be wearing his army uniform. "Going off to save the world," he yelled, as he boarded the train.

Less than a year later, the family would receive the news that his only brother was dead.

Corbin had always felt a responsibility for the death of his brother; he was, after all, his younger brother, and it had been his responsibility to take care of him.

Ella walked to the kitchen and stood behind him. She gently placed her arms around his waist and laid her head in the middle of his back, "Dreams back?" she whispered.

Chapter 18

As he has done for twenty two years, Principal Dilworth began his morning march. The heels of his brown wing-tip oxfords made clicking sounds as he made his way through the hallways of John Logan Bryant High School. Seeing the reflection in the classroom window of a balding, gray-bearded man reminded him of the slender, young, dark-haired man who had come to this job full of enthusiasm and great plans to change the world of education.

"Put your shirt tail in, young man."

"Josh, did you drop that paper? Then pick it up young man."

"No tarrying in the hall young people! Get to class!"

Hugh was surprised to see Principal Dilworth waiting at the double-entry doors when he walked in.

"Good morning, Hugh, could I see you in my office please?" asked Principal Dilworth.

"Yes, sir, do I need to go to homeroom first?" Hugh asked.

"That won't be necessary, just go to my office and I will be there in a few minutes," Principal Dilworth answered. He then turned to a couple leaning against the steel grey lockers, "Young people, close that locker and get to class."

Hugh entered the principal's office and was shocked to find the counselor and a police officer. "Am I in trouble? Do I need to call my parents?" Hugh asked.

"No, son, just have a seat. Principal Dilworth will explain as soon as he gets here." answered the policeman.

Hugh ran his hand through his dark brown hair and sat in one of the three wooden chairs, positioned under the large sliding glass window. He was trying feverishly to think of anything he might have done to cause him to be in trouble with the principal. Surely, he hadn't done anything serious enough that would require the police and the counselor to be there.

Shaking his knees anxiously, Hugh looked up when he heard the stained oak door open.

Principal Dilworth entered, "Sorry to keep you waiting." he said. "Hugh, this is Officer Gregory. He has some questions about Avon Guttenberg."

"Hugh, you know Avon don't you? Avon Guttenberg?" Officer Gregory asked.

"Yes, sir, I have known her since first grade. Is she okay? Is there something wrong with her?" Hugh asked.

"Avon's parents have filed a missing person report with the local police department. They have not seen or heard from her since she left for school on yesterday morning. You and she were friends, is that right?" the officer asked.

"Yes, sir."

"Do you have any idea where she might be? Would she have left voluntarily? Do you know if anything was bothering her?"

"No sir," Hugh lied.

He would never betray Avon's trust. Just as he had shared all his secrets with her, she had depended on his discretion when she had shared the secrets of what went on in her home, the home of Judge Jacob Guttenberg.

Golden curls, dazzling blue eyes and eternally pouty small full lips, Avon Guttenberg, was not only one of the prettiest girls at Bryant High School; she was also one of the smartest. She and Hugh had meet as first graders in Mrs. Adams class of 15 students. They had immediately become competitors for not only Mrs. Adams' attention but for the highest grade in whatever subject they were being tested.

"Okay, Hugh, that's all. Tell Mrs. Stokes to give you a pass to class." Principal Dilworth said.

"You will let us know if you hear anything, won't you son?" Officer Gregory asked.

"Yes, sir, I sure will." Hugh said, standing and reaching for the door knob.

Looking down at the bluish grey, tiled floors as he walked to his class, Hugh remembered walking to class with Avon. Somehow, she was always waiting at his locker before he had gotten there. Like almost every activity, that too, had developed into an undeclared competition. Each morning, Hugh rushed to be at his locker before Avon. Needless to say, with three younger siblings, someone always forgot something and needed to go back for it. He could never be the victor in this competition.

That evening after class, Hugh went straight to the chemistry lab, his and Avon's most favorite place. Without thinking, he had expected to see her sitting at one of the lab stations waiting for him. For the first time ever, she was not there. Hugh was saddened by the thought that she may never be there again.

He smiled as he remembered the fifth grade science fair and how her "aviation-how airplanes fly" had tied for first place with his "solar system display". From that point, they had decided that it was best if they teamed up for future Science Fair Competitions.

When he arrived home that night, he entered the back door to the kitchen. Ella was busy clearing the dishes.

"Hungry?" she asked.

"Yes, what's left?" Hugh replied.

"Your food is in the oven, as usual." Ella answered.

"Mom," Hugh said, getting his plate and sitting at the dinner table. "Would you ever tell someone's secrets?"

"Only if the secret could cause someone harm. I think, that is the only condition under which I would tell a secret. Are you in trouble?" Ella asked.

"No, Mom, I had to report to the principal's office today. There was a policeman there. They had questions about Avon. She is missing since yesterday morning." Hugh replied.

"Well, do you know anything? What did you tell them?"

"All I know is that she talked about leaving. She never told me she was going. She talked about going to California to find her mother. She and her step-mother never really got along."

"God, Justice Guttenberg must be worried to death." Ella responded.

"Yea, I guess." Hugh replied.

"Hugh, what do you mean by that?"

"Nothing. Mom, nothing. I promised the police that if I heard anything that I would let them know."

"And will you?" Ella inquired.

Hugh placed a fork full of food into his mouth and mumbled, "Mmm, sure."

Ella looked at him doubtfully and continued to clean the countertop. Ella finished and left Hugh at the table still eating.

"Wash your dishes before you leave this kitchen," Ella reminded him.

As he sat eating, Hugh thought about the stories Avon had told him about her home life.

A trembling five-year-old Avon sat in her bed with her knees drawn up to her chin listening to the shattering glass outside her door. She could hear her parents yelling, though she could not make out clearly what was being said. There was the sound of more shattered glass and furniture thrown and broken.

The next morning, she made her way down the stairs and into the kitchen. Irene, the cook, was busy making breakfast. "Do you want anything special?" she asked.

"No, where are my parents?" Avon asked

"Your father has left for work. He said that Mrs. Guttenberg had left for a trip."

"Did he say where she went?" Avon asked.

"No, just said she was gone on a trip."

After her mother's departure, Avon spent most nights, sitting with the housekeeper on the long black leather sofa, waiting for her father to get home from work. He usually made it home around nine, sometimes later. Though he was usually already intoxicated, his first stop once home was to the bar.

Mrs. Staples, the live in housekeeper, would take Avon up the stairs and put her to bed, once she had said good night to her father.

"My Avon, my little Avon, all that I have left." The words would slush from Jacob Guttenberg's drunken lips. Then he would kiss her on her forehead and send her off with Mrs. Staples.

One night, after the housekeeper had gone to her quarters over the multi-car garage, Jacob had opened Avon's bedroom door.

"Come and sleep with daddy" he said.

Avon crawled out of her bed and followed her father down the long, royal-blue carpeted hallway, and into her parents' suite. She climbed into her parent's massive custom-made bed of imported Brazilian walnut. Two cherubs playing at the River Avon were hand craved into the headboard, which stretched almost halfway the length of the over thirty-foot wall. Jacob got into bed alongside her and pulled the satin, mauve and teal covers over them both. He took Avon's tiny hand and showed her how to massage his body to satisfaction. Grunting noises came from his side of the bed, as he fell into a drunken sleep.

According to what Avon had shared with Hugh, these nightly visits had continued until she was ten years old. At which time, the Honorable Jacob Guttenberg had found a new bride in the Miss Angel Beckard. Miss Beckard, a twenty year old blonde beauty, was first runner up to the reigning Miss Madison County.

The wedding had been a grand affair, attended by all the local and state dignitaries. The church pews were decorated with imperial purple orchids, pink carnations, million-star gysophilas and white button chrysanthemums, which had been shipped in from Florida.

The five-tier white wedding cake, with golden crème trimming, was made by a famous French baker. The bride's wedding dress had been designed in Paris and shipped to Miss Beckard for sizing, then returned to Paris for final detailing, and returned to Miss Beckard for final approval. Avon joked that the wedding dress had traveled to and from Paris over ten times and still had fewer miles on it than the blushing bride.

When they were in eighth grade, Hugh had asked Avon why she had not reported her father.

Avon replied, "My father is a very powerful man. No one would believe me, and even if they did, they would be afraid to stand up against my father. You forget that Jacob Guttenberg comes from a long line of powerful men."

"But, surely there is someone who can help." Hugh said.

"Who in this county, or state for that matter, has the kind of power of a Guttenberg? And anyway, he has found a new interest in his new bride. As long as he leaves me alone I am okay."

It would be two years before the subject of her father's nocturnal visits were again discussed.

The newspaper announced Judge and Mrs. Jacob Guttenberg has become the parents of two beautiful twin boys. Matthew and Mark, identical twin sons, were born at eleven thirty two on April 1, 1938.

Avon told Hugh that her father had returned to drinking heavily, almost as soon as his new bride had announced her pregnancy. Avon had locked her bedroom door but to no avail; her father had removed the lock. She had spent many nights sleeping on the bathroom floor, because it still had a lockable door.

The night before her disappearance, Hugh who slept on a cot in the front room, had heard a tapping at the window above his bed. He pulled back the curtains to see Avon peeping into the window. He sneaked to the front door and opened it to let her in.

“I’m leaving,” she said.

“Leaving, when?” Hugh asked.

“Tonight, I wanted to come by and say goodbye.”

“Do you need anything? Are you sure this is the right thing to do?”

“Yes, I can’t stay in that house another day. He said that if I told anyone, or tried to leave, he would have me put into an institution for the mentally insane. And I believe that he would do it.” Avon said.

“Then wait a minute,” Hugh said, walking to the closet and opening the door. He bent down and pulled out a small metal box. He opened the lid of the box and handed Avon an envelope filled with money. “I want you to have this”

“No” Avon said,” I have some money saved.”

“I want to make sure you have all the money that you need. I could never rest if I thought that you were out there someplace stranded.” Hugh urged.

“Okay, but I will pay you back as soon as I can. And as soon as I am settled, I will write to you.” Avon said, grabbing on to Hugh and hugging him tightly, she said,”I love you, you are my best friend. Promise me you will never tell anyone.”

“I promise,” Hugh said.

Hugh watched as Avon walked off the porch and into the night headed for the bus station in town.

Chapter 19

After classes, Anna liked to stop by the home economics teachers' classroom. She liked helping her clean and put away the tools and materials of the day. But mostly, she enjoyed the conversations they shared. Anna was a talented seamstress and could one day become a great designer, Mrs. Montgomery had said.

Mrs. Montgomery had taught at John Logan Bryant High School for five years. She was from Philadelphia. She was the first person that Anna had ever met from so far away. Anna loved the way she talked. She sounded so refined, so different from the other teachers on staff. She admired the way Mrs. Montgomery carried herself, tall and slender like mama, but there was a swing to her walk, uncommon for the women of the Grove. Her dark brown hair hung to her shoulders, with bangs cut just above her well-arched eyebrows. Her white blouse and slim black skirt followed the curves of her body perfectly.

As they worked to clean up the classroom, Mrs. Montgomery mentioned that her husband was opening a new drugstore in town. He was looking to hire a student to help him with getting setup. The position would become permanent part-time once business picked up.

Anna was excited by the idea. "Please tell him about me. Please!"

Mrs. Montgomery assured Anna that she would speak to her husband. She was aware that Anna came from a large family and that the family had four children attending high school at the same time. The money, she was sure, would come in handy.

Passing by the full length mirror on the classroom wall, Anna was again reminded of how she had been denied the traits of her mother's natural beauty. Her limp, yellowish brown hair hang loosely in a ponytail at the back of her neck. Her long torso and short legs made her look frog-like, she thought. Aileen and Amy both had the gift of her mother's shapely body including the sleek long legs. For a minute, she felt the burn of jealousy, then clearing her thoughts, how could she be jealous of her sisters. How could anyone be jealous of their own sisters? She thought.

True to her word, Mrs. Montgomery had spoken to her husband. He agreed to hire Anna, and two weeks later, she was in the stock room learning the ins and outs of being an assistant to a pharmacist.

Anna, now a senior, had classes until 12 noon. She would leave the campus and stop by the burger shop and then report to work at precisely 1pm. She would initially work 5 hours, and if things picked up, her hours would be increased. Anna was overjoyed at having such a responsible position.

A month later, Anna running late, stopped at the burger shop to get a sandwich to take with her to work. She had gone by Mrs. Montgomery's classroom that day and had stayed longer than anticipated. She sat at the counter, waiting for Sandy, one of her classmates who worked at the burger shop after school, to come out and serve her. Instead, a man a bit older than she, appeared on the other side of the counter. "Can I help you?" he asked.

"Does Sandy still work here?" she asked.

"Yes, he's in back. Hi my name is Vic. I'm the new owner." he said, while lifting his muscular arm offering his hand to shake hers.

Anna could tell from the well-defined muscles under his indigo tee shirt that he was a man who took care of his body.

“Yes, I’d like a corned beef sandwich to go, please… and a pickle.”

“Okay, a corned beef sandwich coming up. Just how do you like your pickles, Miss?”

Anna couldn’t hide the flush of red on her cheeks. She wasn’t used to men making small talk, and she thought, “I think this guy is flirting with me.” Anna started to twist on the swivel seat as she waited for her order to be prepared.

Returning with her food in a bag, the man handed it to her, holding on to the bag just long enough to touch her hand. A smile she could not stop eased across her lips. ”Thank you,” she said. getting down from the stool and dashing out the door.

While dressing for school the following morning, Amy asked, “Anna are you wearing lipstick?”

“Why?”

“Nothing, it looks good on you. You should try something new with your hair. I just love the new bob cut that Gloria Swanson wore in her last movie. And you…

“Please don’t try to tell me how to wear my hair. If I want to cut it, I will.”

Unable to understand the changes taking place in Anna’s attitude, Amy got dressed for school and went out to catch the bus, which was just rounding the curve at the end of the street. Amy sat in the empty seat next to her twin. Anna sat in silence, reading from a Life Magazine, which Mrs. Montgomery had given her. Amy pulled the college applications from her bag and began to study them.

“Will I see you at lunch?” Amy asked, as the bus approached the tar-covered circular drive in front of the main building.

"No, I'll grab a sandwich at the café and go straight to work."

"Okay then, I'll see you at home this evening. Try to get home on time. Dad and Mom are concerned about you getting in so late."

"Okay, see you at home." Anna replied.

As she approached the café for lunch, Anna noticed the new sign above the café door. VIC's is shown in bold red letters. In the large front window, a sign proclaimed "Under New Management- Best sandwiches in town".

Anna went inside and sat on her customary stool at the counter. She noticed that the old furniture had been replaced by six new green Formica-topped tables, with chrome legged and four matching chairs for each.

Almost immediately, Vic appeared behind the counter.

"I see you've made some changes," she said.

Smiling he replied, "Yes. What do you think?"

"I see you chose table tops to compliment your eyes. Is that a personal statement of some kind?"

They both smiled.

"One corned beef sandwich and a large pickle, right?" Vic asked.

Returning with Anna's order, Vic asked, "Hey, what are you doing later this evening?"

"I work at Montgomery's Drugstore until 6, and then I usually walk home."

"Why don't you let me pick you up, today? I could give you a ride."

At six o'clock, Anna said good night to Dr. Montgomery and headed to the front door. As she was turning the sign hanging on the door from open to the side that said closed, she noticed a black four- door car parked out front. Stepping out onto the sidewalk, she recognized the driver as Vic from the café.

"I'm here to take you home, Madame," he said, going to the passenger's side to open the door.

"Persistent, aren't we? "Anna chided, taking a seat inside the car.

On the drive home, Anna thought, I can't let him meet Amy yet. Thinking to herself, Anna felt sure that if Vic were to meet Amy, he would be unable to control himself. He would surely end his pursuit of her and, instead choose to go after the pretty Amy.

Anna decided then that she was not ready for Vic to meet her family. She directed Vic to drop her at the mailboxes at the end of her street; she would walk home from there.

Walking home from the mailbox, Anna remembered all the boys she had liked and how they had, instead, pursued Amy: Billy from the church choir, who Amy had no interest in, even as he trailed behind her like a lap dog, Jamie, quarterback for the football teams, Amy knew that I adored him, she thought, even as he sent Valentines candy to her, and she said he was too childish.

This one, she thought, Amy will not get; this one is all mine.

Each day at 6pm Vic's car would be parked in front of the drug store. Leaning against the hood, he would go to the passenger side door and hold it open for Anna as she got inside.

On the drive home, she learned that Vic had grown up not far from Clover Grove. He had opted to join the army at 17, instead of finishing high school. He had been in the military for the past 6 years. He had traveled extensively and had used his military savings to buy and remodel the café.

Listening as Vic talked about all the exotic places that he had traveled, like Russia, India, Australia, excited Anna. She had never talked about it much, but it was her dream to travel the world, just as it was Carlton's. She could almost hear her parents say, "Travel the world, stick with reality, Anna." as if she had no right to dream of something bigger and better than the Grove. They would never, ever tell Aileen or Amy to stop dreaming.

One evening as Anna was closing the door to the drugstore, she noticed that Vic's car was not parked outside. "Well, it was bound to end, she thought, as she began her walk home." As she approached the corner, she could see Vic's car coming over the hill. He pulled the car over and parked next to her and got out.

"Sorry, I'm late," he said. Reaching inside the car, he hand her a bouquet of pink and lavender flowers. Tilting her head down, so that he could not see the water developing in the corners of her eyes she smiled, "Thanks."

"Can we go for a drive before I take you home?" Vic asked. "There is something I'd like to show you."

"Why not?" Anna replied.

Vic turned the car toward Ferguson Lake. They parked in one of the picnic areas.

"Come on," Vic said, headed to the car trunk. He took a wicker picnic basket and a blanket from the trunk and walked over to one of the picnic tables. He spread the blanket over the table and took a plate of sandwiches, two long stemmed glasses and a bottle of wine from the basket.

"We're celebrating," he said, lifting Anna by her waist and placing her atop the wooden picnic table.

"Celebrating what?" Anna asked.

"The very first time you walked into my new business and changed my life," Vic responded, handing Anna a small plate and a wine glass, and then taking a seat beside her. "It's been a month you know."

"A month," Anna mused, as if she had not lived and relived each and every activity of each and every minute that they had spent together.

Vic placed a diagonally-cut half corned beef sandwich on Anna's plate and handed it to her. He then filled the two wine glasses. The taste of wine was not unfamiliar to Anna; she had had the odd glass at New Year's Eve and other such family gatherings. But this wine was different. She couldn't figure out if it was the wine or the occasion that was causing the distinction. This, indeed, was the best wine she had ever tasted.

They sat and talked of Vic's plans for the café. One day, he said, he wanted to own a French Restaurant. He reminisced about all the French foods that he had eaten while in France and about how fancy the French people dressed to go out to eat. Anna was so impressed with how easily the French words like Blanquette de Veau, Soupe à L'oignon flowed from his lips. She watched as his lip formulated each word. He has prefect lips, she thought.

Anna was mesmerized as he spoke.

Suddenly, he reached over and took her glass. Leaning back onto the blanketed table, he pulled her back with him. Slowly he placed his lips to hers. Anna was caught off guard when he slipped his tongue between her lips. She and Amy had talked about tongue kissing before, but this was a first for her. Vic guided her tongue into his mouth and began a gentle sucking. Anna thought, surely this is what heaven feels like. The sweet fruity taste of the wine was on his lips. Anna felt she could swallow his lips. Vic was holding her so close, she began to shiver in his arms. Vic rolled over on top of Anna still holding her tightly.

I love you, I love you, I love you so. Anna mouthed, nonverbally into Vic's ear.

So focused on the kiss, Anna had not noticed that Vic had opened his pants and was lying between her legs. Her skirt pushed to one side. She felt a pinch, then absolute pleasure. Heaven…………… she thought……..Heaven.

For a month, Vic would be at the drugstore waiting to drive Anna home. The trip usually ending at the lake or some out-of-the way spot along the highway and usually involved some kind of alcoholic drink.

Business at the café was picking up and on some evenings Vic was not able to come to the drugstore to pick Anna up. Anna didn't mind, she would walk the three blocks to the café. Vic had installed a new Wurlitzer; with the drop of a nickel, it would light up and then an arm would pull down the chosen record. The needle would drop on the plastic record and the place would start to jump. Anna liked listening to Bing Cosby, Frank Sinatra and Nat King Cole. She enjoyed the sounds and the smells of the café, watching the people, but mostly, she enjoyed the time she spent with Vic.

On evening, Anna had taken particular care in dressing for Vic. She knew that his favorite color on her was red. She had carefully chosen a red V-neck sweater with small pearl like buttons down the front. She borrowed Amy's slim, black knee length shirt, because it looked so much like the skirts that Mrs. Montgomery wore. She wore stockings with a black seam down the back of her legs and black pumps. She left the drugstore and walked the three blocks to the café.

The usual crowd was there and a few new people. The Wurlitzer was going full blast; she took her usual seat at the counter. Vic looked over at her and gave her a grin. She blushed.

Vic asked if she wanted anything to eat. She said no but she would like a soda. Vic went to the back and brought back a glass filled. "Special soda, just for my lady," he said.

With the first sip, Anna could taste the bourbon. The more she drank the happier she became. She went to the center of the floor and started to dance alone.

Floyd Channing, a once handsome man and known around town as a quick tempered womanizer, took Anna's hand and pulled her in tight to him. She pushed him away. Floyd became angry and pulled her in even harder.

Vic came from behind the counter and stood between Anna and Floyd. " Floyd, I don't think the lady wants to dance with you," Vic said.

Floyd reached around Vic and caught on to Anna's wrist, pulling her to him. Vic pushed Floyd, and the two men began to tussle. Floyd, a good 25 pounds heavier than Vic, knocked Vic to the floor. Vic picked up a soda bottle that had fallen to the floor, getting up from the floor, he lifted the glass bottle and slammed it against Floyd's head, blood dripped from Floyd's head and face. There was a big gash on Floyd's head and a cut across his face. Floyd grabbed paper napkins from the table and applied them to his bloody face.

"Get out of my business and don't ever come back!" Vic yelled.

Floyd holding the paper napkins to his face promised Vic that he would definitely hear from him again. "This is not over," Floyd yelled, while being helped into a waiting car parked outside.

Anna was convinced that she loved Vic. Even though he had not said so, she was sure that this proved that he loved her also.

One afternoon after classes, she stopped in to return some borrowed magazine to Mrs. Montgomery.

"Dr. Montgomery tells me you are doing great at the drugstore," Mrs. Montgomery said.

"You are so lucky to have married Dr. Montgomery. He is so smart, kind and willing to help. He has taught me so much in such a short period of time. I can't remember if I have said it before but thank you again for recommending me."

"I don't know that luck had anything to do with it; truth is, marriage is a lot of work. Dr. Montgomery and I were married before he graduated college, which meant, for a while, I was our only source of income. But he has made up for that, many times over. He is a good man. I hope someday you will find a good man to marry. And yes, this is the third time you have thanked me. So please, no more thanks needed. Just learn as much as you can and try to enjoy the work."

Anna left Mrs. Montgomery's classroom and headed for Vic's to get her corned beef sandwich for lunch, before heading to work.

Anna walked inside and the café door closed behind her. Approaching her usual stool at the counter, she took her yellow and blue checkered scarf from around her neck and placed it into her bag. She then looks up to see the most beautiful creature she had ever seen.

The creature was standing behind the counter. She was so tiny that, at first Anna thought she was a child in dress up. Her skin was flawlessly clear. Thick, glossy, black hair hung to her waist. Her dark almond-shaped eyes were bright and clear. She was holding napkins in her doll-like hands. Anna could tell that she was Asian, but could not tell from what country.

"Hello," Anna said, "is Vic here?"

"Vic, Vic, my husband," smiling, the beautiful creature responded. "Wait here, please."

Coming from the back room, carrying a blue plastic tray filled with drinking glasses, Vic's eyes went from Anna to the creature. He walked over to the creature behind the counter and smiled. "Honey, this is Anna, she is one of our best customers."

Anna stood with her mouth open. She couldn't believe what she was hearing or seeing. Just last night, just last night….She couldn't even complete the thought. Words were there, but she couldn't seem to find them. The words were whirling around her head. She could almost see them but couldn't snatch the right ones to say. She didn't know what she felt: anger, hurt, confused, used… stupid. Suddenly the bottom of her stomach was in her throat. She knew that if she stood there one minute longer, she would throw up. She would not give him the satisfaction of seeing her do anything so immature.

She turned and ran through the door and down the street, running to no place in particular. There was no place to go, there was no place she needed to be, and there was no place she wanted to be, no place …without Vic. So she just ran.

Breathlessly, Anna found herself on a familiar corner. She walked over to a man leaning against a non-distinct brick building. Dressed in a brown zoot suit, he looked like a character from one of Hugh's cartoon magazines. She handed him three dollars, a transaction she had seen Vic make many times over the past several months. Stuffing the bills into his pant pocket, the man left and returned with a brown paper bag containing a liquid in a pint sized bottle. Anna took the bottle and put it in her bag, then walked away to find a place of solitude.

A week later, Anna was leaving the drug store, parked outside she saw Vic's car. She stepped out to the sidewalk and began her walk home. Vic ran to catch up with her.

"Just let me explain" he said, taking her by the elbow. "I never meant to hurt you. I never meant to fall in love with you. Please, Anna, let me explain."

Anna looked at him with defeated eyes.

"What do you want Vic? You are a married man. You could have at least told me. You could have let me decide if I wanted to be with a married man, but you didn't. You took that choice away from me along with my dignity."

Anna turned to walk away, Vic caught her by the arm, "Anna listen, I had planned to tell you. Honestly I had."

"Honest, honest, that should be the last word to come out of your mouth, Vic. You were not honest to me or to your wife."

"Listen, baby," Vic continued, "Ah Lam has been out of the country for six months. She went home to visit her mom. When I met you, I had no idea that I would fall in love with you. I thought we would just be friends, but then I fell in love with you."

"And your wife, AA Lom, is it Vic, do you love your wife?" Anna sneered.

"Ah ....ah Anna, I'm just confused right now. Can we get into the car and talk about it? Please Anna, just give me a few minutes. I know you are angry and hurt, but, Baby just give me a few minutes," Vic said, guiding Anna toward the open passenger door.

Vic got in on the driver's side and steered the car toward Ferguson Lake. He parked the car, went to Anna's side and opened the door, gently taking her hand he led her to a familiar picnic table. He lifted her by her waist and sat her softly on the table top. Standing between her legs he bent his long body to kiss her lips.

With one hand, he gently brushed her hair from her face, then allowed his hand to travel to the nape of her neck, while whispering into her ear, "Please forgive me Anna, I love you so. I can't live without you."

Hungrily kissing her lips, he leans into her. Allowing his free hand to deal with the business of clothing, their bodies fell back onto the table. And once again, Anna was in Heaven.

Chapter 20

Watching adoringly as Quinn tried to pull, then push Lilla up the sloping hill in his red, four-wheeled wagon, Aileen said, “Mom, I think I’ll take Quinn to town to get new shoes today. He is walking right out of the ones he is wearing.”

The red wagon with aero flyer painted in white beneath golden wings on both sides, had quickly become Quinn’s favorite toy. As soon as Grandpa had given it to him, It had also become the source of constant disputes between he and Lilla.

“Sure,” Ella replied. “Hey, do you mind taking Lilla? She could really use a new pair of shoes for church. Those two are growing like weeds.”

Later that day, Aileen, Quinn and Lilla were leaving Skienners Family Shoes, when Quinn spotted an ice cream cone sign in one of the glass front windows.

“Can we go in and get some ice cream” Quinn asked.

“Me too,” chimed Lilla,” I want ice cream, too.”

Seeing that she was outnumbered, “Okay,” Aileen agreed. Centering herself between the two, she took each by the hand. They walked in under the big red sign “Vic’s. A tiny bell rang as she opened the door, and all three looked up to see where the sound had come from.

Standing behind the counter was a man; she recognized him immediately. He had aged some, gained a little weight; the long narrow face with the arrow-pointed chin had grown more muscular, but the green devil eyes were the same. He would never be able to change those devil green eyes, and she would never forget them. Victor, Victor Beasley, rapist.

She turned to Quinn, who by now had locked green eyes to green eyes with Victor.

Grabbing both children by an arm, Aileen backed out the door and began to walk as fast as she could to get back to the car.

"What's wrong Mom? What about the ice cream, Mom?" Quinn squealed.

Struggling to keep up, Lilla fell to the sidewalk, she was in tears, gurgling something about promised ice cream she never ever got.

Aileen looked around and, for a minute, couldn't remember where she had parked the car.

"Mom, are you alright?" Quinn was saying to deaf ears, "Mom, are you alright? Mommy are you alright?" Finally, the fog began to clear, and Aileen could hear her son's voice coming from somewhere distant.

"Yes, baby, I'm alright. Everything is alright." She looked down at Lilla's tear-stained face, took a white handkerchief from her purse, and gently wiped her face.

"Aunt Aileen is so sorry, Lilla. Are you hurt?" Examining Lilla for any injuries, Aileen repeated, "Are you both okay?" Lilla's newly purchased shoes showed evidence of her struggle to keep up, the toes were badly scuffed.

In that moment, she missed Michael more than she had the entire time that she and Quinn had been in Clover Grove. She needed, she thought, her husband.

"We will have to go back to the shoe store and replace Lilla's shoes, then we will stop at the store and get enough ice cream for everybody. You, me, Lilla and everybody at home. We will make this a celebration."

"What kind of celebration?" Asked Lilla.

"Celebrating New Shoes Day," replied Aileen.

Bang, bang, bang! "Who's in the restroom?" Amy yelled. "Hey, whoever is in there, come out. I need to get dressed too."

Opening the bathroom door, Anna came out wiping her face, with a wash cloth. "Good God, I was only in there a few minutes"

Amy looked at Anna's flushed face and said, "What the heck happened to you? You look like hell."

"None of your business," Anna replied, passing Amy to get into their bedroom.

At the breakfast table, the conversation was lively. Amy was ecstatically waving an envelope she had received from the University. She had been accepted. Of all the applications she had sent out, this was the one she was hoping would be accepted. Only fifty miles from home, just far enough to establish some independence, and close enough to get home once a month or so.

"And get this, she boasted, a full four year scholarship in the department of Music Appreciation!"

"That's great," Carlton congratulated Amy. "If I get an ROTC scholarship, I'll be able to attend university with you next year."

“ROTC, what’s that,” asked Corbin.

“It stands for Reserve Officers Training Corp.”, answered Carlton.” It’s a military training program offered at the college. The recruiter said that I was sure to get in. He said that if I complete the program, then I would become an army officer.”

“Okay, enough about that for the morning,” injected Ella, trying desperately to deflect an argument, so early in the morning.

Anna entered the kitchen took a seat at the table, and looked over at the half-cooked eggs on Hugh’s plate, the yellow yolk running over the side of the plate. She bolted for the back door. Amy got up and followed her outside.

“Damn, Hugh and his runny eggs, why can’t he eat his eggs cooked like everybody else.” Anna said, bending to finish emptying her stomach on to the clover covered ground on the side of the house.

“Are you sick, Anna?” Amy asked.

“What do you mean?”

“I mean, are you pregnant?”

Anna had been feeling terrible the last week or so, but thought she was coming down with flu or something, not once had she considered that she might be pregnant.

“I don’t know,” Anna said. ”I guess I could be.”

“Amy please, please, don’t tell Mama. Please don’t tell Papa. Give me some time to think this through. Please!” Anna said, crying into her hands.

“Who’s the father?” Amy asked, “Do you know who the father is?”

Anna incensed by the implication, said through gritted teeth, "If I'm pregnant, yes I know who the father is. There can only be one father."

"Who is he?" Amy again asked.

Wiping her face with the tail of her pink robe, Anna walked pass Amy, opened the back door, which made a slamming sound as she hurried pass the kitchen and into her bedroom.

Okay, I'll be at the drugstore when you get off today. But I have to get back to the café early; tonight is a busy night." Vic whispered into the telephone receiver.

At 6pm, Vic's car was parked outside the drugstore. Anna walked over to the passenger side door, opened it, and got inside.

"Can we go someplace? I really need to talk to you." Anna said.

"Okay, but remember I have to get back," replied Vic. turning the car toward Ferguson Lake.

Vic parked the car then turned to pull Anna over for a kiss. Anna held up her hand to stop him. "Vic, we really need to talk. I'm pregnant. "

"Are you sure?" Vic asked, turning in his seat to face the steering wheel. "Whose is it? Is it mine?"

Anna felt shocked then angry at Vic's question. "What do you mean is it yours, Vic?"

"I'm sorry baby, I was just caught by surprise. I know that if you are pregnant, the baby is mine. What do you want to do?"

"What do I want to do? What the hell does that mean, Vic? What are we going to do, Vic? Remember, you said that you were going to divorce Ah Lam, as soon as you could. You said as soon as she had been in this country long enough, you were going to leave her. You said she only wanted to stay married long enough to meet permanent residency requirement. So how much longer will that take?"

"I'm working on it, baby. It won't be much longer, trust me. You do trust me, right? We can work this out. You and I will work this out so that we can be together," Vic assured Anna.

"As soon as I settle this thing with Ah Lam, I'll be free, and then we can get married and raise our child together. We will work together at the café. Next month when you graduate, we will announce our engagement," Vic promised.

"You know that I love you don't you, baby?" leaning over to kiss her. This time, Anna's lips were receptive.

Vic whispered," Baby, you know I can't live without you, don't you?"

Taking Anna by the waist, he slid her down so that she was lying on the car's front seat. He continued kissing her more aggressively. Wrapped in Vic's caresses, Anna forgot about the argument, promises, Ah Lam, and the pregnancy. For the moment, Anna was taking another trip to Heaven.

Walking home from work the next day, Anna was focused on her coming engagement to Vic. Aileen and Amy and the rest of the family would be so surprised to find out that she had been secretly dating, not only a very handsome man, but also a businessman in his own right. She would wait a month later, before announcing the pregnancy. Vic was taking care of everything, he had told her so. All she needed to do was concentrate on staying healthy and graduating next month.

So focused was she that she did not notice Bethel sitting behind the screened-in porch.

“Hey there, is that you Anna? How is your mom doing? I haven’t seen her or your dad in a month or so. I heard Aileen was back in town.”

“Oh, hello, Cousin Beth, how are you? And how is Cousin Henry?” “Momma and Papa are both doing just fine.”

“Yeah, I heard Aileen was back in town and she had a baby. Is that right, she has a son. I sure thought she would have come by to see me once she was in town. She has a baby, is that right?”

“Yes, Cousin Beth, Aileen and her son have been here a little over two months now. I will tell her that you asked about her and would like to see her and meet her son, Quinn.”

“Quinn, that’s his name? That’s a strange name for a boy.

“Hey did you hear what happened at that café in town, that Vic’s place?” Bethel continued. “They tell me there was a fight and Floyd Channing got hurt really bad. Those Channing boys shouldn’t be messed with. That Jacobs boy hasn’t been heard from since he had a fight with that youngest Channing boy. That Vic had better be careful, if he wants to see his child born.”

Anna stopped dead in her track, “How could Beth know? Who else knows? Amy must have told her. She promised not to tell.”

“You know, that little Chinese wife of his is pregnant,” Beth continued, “That Jacobs boy was a mean one too,” she continued, murmuring to herself. “Lord, Lord, you just don’t know what’s on young people’s minds.”

Anna felt like she had been hit in her stomach. She refused to let Beth she her flinch. She didn’t know how much Beth knew, whether she had spoken with the intent of hurting her, or just being her regular nosy self, bargaining for more information by offering what she had already heard.

“Cousin Beth, I have to go. Tell Cousin Henry that I said hello,” Anna said, rushing, almost galloping, to get home.

Stumbling into the back door, Anna went directly to her bedroom and closed the door. Falling onto the bed, she placed the pillow to her face, biting down on the pillow so hard that she felt the shafts of the feathers break between her teeth. She wailed into the pillow; so violent were her convulsive sobs that she could feel the bed vibrate beneath her.

It was dark outside when Anna approached the car shed. She stopped for a minute to remember the many nights spent lying flat like canned sardine on the front porch, star gazing and storytelling.

Hugh would always be the first to spot the North Star and finger pointed to the sky, pick out and name the constellations, while everyone else struggled to see them.

Mom would tell stories of life with her mother and three siblings, after their father had abandoned them for some distant dream and how, even as a single mother, her mom had provided for them and sent them as far in school as they had wanted to go.

Then everyone would laugh at one of Amy's adventures, like the time she got stuck in the huge drainage pipe under Hwy 47. And how Anna, Carlton and Hugh were afraid to go for help for fear of the punishment they would get for being "anywhere near that highway".

A hint of a smile crept at the edge of Anna lips as she entered the wide doorway used by Corbin to drive in the automobiles and tractors for repair. The heavy iron chain used to lift the door hung against the wall.

Corbin was lying on his back underneath Mr. McClinton old red truck. Anna said nothing as she bent forward and leaned against the open hood of the truck. From underneath the truck, Corbin could see Anna's black sneakered feet. He recognized the slightly inward turned pigeon toes immediately.

"Hey, baby girl," he said.

"Hi, Daddy," Anna responded. Moving over to the work bench, she inspected the tools lying there. Without thinking, she began to organize them by size and shapes into neat piles, wrenches, pliers, nuts and sockets. A roll of paper napkins was lying on the bench. Anna tore a napkin from the roll and began wiping down all the tools and the workbench.

Finished, she moved to the vise attached to the edge of the work bench, a favorite since childhood. Over and over, she spun the vise tight then released it, as she had done many times as a child.

The old wood burning heater that Corbin and the boys had built had been relegated to the far corner of the shed for the spring and summer months. Anna was reminded of the many cold nights her father had spent alone in the car shed, lying on his back under others people's cars.

“I guess I’ll go back inside” she said, “by the way Momma wants to know how soon you will be in.”

“In about thirty-minutes, tell her, as soon as I can get this muffler tightened.”

In this thirty-minute visit, so few words had been spoken, but so much had been said to remind Anna of who she was and where she belonged. As she returned to the house, she knew what she had to do.

Chapter 21

Anna telephoned Vic. She needed to talk to him, she said, but not on the telephone party lines. She needed to see him in person. Vic agreed to be at the drugstore when she left work.

As she was closing the door to the drugstore, she saw Vic standing next to his car.

"Vic, I have made some decisions, I am not going to have the baby. I realize there is no future for you and me. I don't want to complicate things any further," she said, turning to walk away.

At this, Vic bearishly grabbed her arm and turned her to face him. "What do you mean, you decided not to have my baby? Who said you could decide? It's my baby, and I will decide what happens to it," he said, with his alcohol laced breath, staring in Anna's eyes, almost nose to nose.

"Vic, I know about your wife and her pregnancy. It's ludicrous to think that you and I have any kind of future. I just want to get on with my life and let you get on with yours," Anna said.

"You can't make decisions for me. I make decisions for you. And if you know what's good for you, you will stop thinking about doing anything without my permission. Is that clear? Now get into the car," Vic said, while pushing her into the passenger seat.

They did not speak the entire drive to Ferguson Lake.

"Get out and get into the back seat," Vic ordered. Anna rebelled, pulling away from his grip of her arms. Vic pulled her from the front seat, threw her into the back seat, and fell on top of her. This time there was no Heaven as Vic continued to pleasure himself at her expense.

The silence was so absolute on the drive home, that Anna could hear the tire treads rhythmically beating against the highway pavement. As the car neared the mailboxes on Hwy 47 where Anna normally got out, Vic turned to her and said, "I'm sorry; you know that I love you, don't you?"

"I'll always love you, and I just can't live without you. You know that don't you, baby?"

"Anna, Anna, you know that don't you? I can't live without you," Vic pled.

"Goodnight, Vic" Anna said, as she got out of the car, stepped onto the black tar paved road, and began the journey home.

"Are you sure?" Amy asked, sitting on the twin bed.

"Yes, I have decided," Anna said. "I heard about a place over in Peterson County that does it for a hundred and fifty dollars. It will take half of my savings but I have made up my mind to get it done."

"What's mama going to say?" Amy asked.

"I haven't talked to mama. You are the only one who knows. If mama knew, you know what she would say. So it's best that she and papa don't know. This has to stay between you and me. Okay?"

"Okay," Amy replied, getting up from the bed and hugging Anna tightly. "Me and you."

Because abortion was illegal in the 1930s, Anna knew that, if caught, both she and the doctor performing the abortion could be charged with a crime. She and Amy both knew of the seriousness of what they were about to do.

According to the instructions, Anna was to arrive after 7pm. She was to park in front of a gray two story building on the corner of Walnut St. and College Ave. She was to wait there until someone came for her.

Sitting in the car, Amy behind the steering wheel and Anna in the passenger side, they tried to calm each other's fears.

Anna said "It's going to be okay," looking at the worry lines on Amy's face. I have researched everything. I have talked to girls at school who have had it done before. They say this is the best place, that's why it costs so much. I'm going to be fine," Anna said, more to herself than anyone else.

Suddenly a car pulled up behind them, the headlights were almost blinding, shining in the rear view mirror. Amy grabbed Anna's hand. They instantly read the others thoughts: "police".

Someone in the car behind them opened the door and got out of the car. Anna and Amy strained to see who it was but couldn't. The headlights were too bright.

A woman's voice outside of the passenger door said, "Which one of you is it." Anna replied, "It's me."

"Get out and come with me," the woman directed. Anna started to get out of the car and so did Amy. "Only her," the woman said.

"It's okay" Anna said to Amy.

Amy continued collecting her purse, the keys and her scarf, "There is no way on this earth that you are going without me," Amy scoffed.

Looking around, and not wanting to waste any more time, the woman, relented, "Okay, both of you get in the back seat of my car."

Once in the backseat, both Anna and Amy were handed blindfolds. "Here, put these on and keep them on until I bring you back to your car."

After about a ten-minute drive, the driver's door opened, the woman and another person helped both Anna and Amy inside a heavy door. The smell of alcohol and antiseptics permeated the room. Holding hands, they were escorted to a bench against the wall and directed to sit.

From under her blindfold Anna could see white women's nursing shoes. The woman came over and took Anna gently by the hand, "Do you have the money?"

Anna reached into her pocket and pulled out a wad of twenty and ten dollar bills. The woman took the money and disappeared, reappearing minutes later with a man whose white shoes Anna could also see under her blind fold.

The two took Anna one on either side and guided her to a table. Following the hands guiding her, Anna lay back on the table and put each of her legs into a stirrup. She had been told earlier that she need not wear any under garments.

The procedure took less than twenty minutes. Somehow, a pad had been placed strategically between her legs to control bleeding. Anna felt faint, she felt like she needed to rest a bit. But she was hurriedly helped down from the table, and she and Amy were escorted back outside to the waiting car.

They were then driven, still blindfolded, back to where they had left their car. They were helped into the car and told not to take the blind folds off until they heard the car drive off.

"Are you alright," Amy asked worriedly.

"I'm alright, but can we just sit here a minute? I feel a little weak."

"Are you hurting, do you need to lie down?" Amy asked.

"Here get into the back seat and lie down."

Too weak to protest, Anna complied and crawled into the back seat. Amy took the long scarf from her purse folded it and put it under Anna's head. She took Anna's scarf and laid it across Anna's upper body.

"Now rest, Anna, while I get us home," Amy said.

For three days, Anna did not leave her bedroom except to go to the bathroom to check for bleeding. Whenever Anna was able to eat, Amy made sure that she had food and lots of liquids, as the abortion nurse had recommended on the drive back to their car. It proved to be a difficult task, but Amy worked diligently to insure that the younger girls spent as little time as possible in their shared bedroom.

Amy tapped the tiny gold tone metal bell again. Stumbling over a small stack of brown cardboard boxes, Dr. Montgomery peeked out of the window-like opening, which served as the drop off and pickup area for his customers.

"Oh, hello," he said, dressed in a crisp white shirt and thin black tie under his white knee length lab coat.

"I'm sorry, my assistant is out today, and I have to try to stand in for her. I have to say though, I'm a little rusty and out of my element in this area," he admitted, pushing his round frame tortoise shell glasses back from the tip of his narrow nose with one hand, while holding a clipboard and pencil in his other hand.

"That's okay," Amy said, "as a matter of fact that's why I'm here."

I'm Anna's sister, Amy, Amy Sumpner. Anna is my twin sister. Anyway Anna is not feeling well. She sent me to tell you that she would not be in today. She hasn't been well for the past couple of days."

"Sorry to hear that, nothing serious, I hope," replied Dr. Montgomery, empathically.

"No," Amy replied, trying to be as discreetly delicate as possible. "It's something we women have to deal with. It's a part of being a woman; it's just a more difficult part for some women than others."

"I'm glad to hear that it's not something too serious. I don't know how I would survive around here without her. Is there anything she needs?" he asked.

Trapped in his steel gray eyes, Amy thought he looked nothing like Anna had described him. He was a youngish thirty something. Curls played at his ears even though his curly black hair was cut razor sharp at the arch behind his ears and at his neckline. Dashing, Amy thought, is how she would describe him. Yeah, dashingly handsome, that's how I would describe him.

"Here, wait a minute, let me look," he said, laying down the clipboard and studying one shelf then the next. He pulled a small box from the shelf and handed it to Amy.

Amy took the small pink box with two angels lying on fluffy white clouds.

Dr. Montgomery said, "Tell her to take two of these pills with water once every four to six hours. I have it on good authority that these will work wonderfully for relieving that kind of pain."

"Thank you," Anna said, as she turned and headed for the door. "I'm sure she will appreciate it and will be back to work in a couple of days."

"Feeling any better?" Amy asked, as she entered and closed the bedroom door.

Lying under the tattered Dutch doll-patterned quilt, which had been on their beds since they were six years old, Anna answered, "Still weak, but getting there. Has mom said anything yet?"

"Not yet, but I expect, it any minute. You know nothing much gets past Ella Sumpner. But don't worry; I'll take care of it."

In the kitchen preparing school lunches for Dana, Lorraine and Grace. "What's going on with Anna?" Ella asked, "She hasn't been out of her bedroom in two days."

"Nothing much," Amy answered, "just monthly stuff, having a rough go this month. I already spoke to her teachers and Dr. Montgomery," Amy said, leaning in and kissing Ella on the cheek. "She will be okay," Amy added, while leaving through the back door to get to the bus stop.

After three days in her bedroom, Anna emerged from her bedroom door. She walked down the hall toward the bathroom. Ella spotted her moving gingerly down the hallway.

"Anna, are you alright," Ella asked. "Do you need to see the doctor?"

"No, Momma, I am fine, I had an unusually bad cycle, but I'm getting better; as a matter of fact, I think I will be able to go to school and to work tomorrow."

Knowingly, Ella walked toward Anna and kissed her on her forehead, "If you need to talk, I'm here. Your dad and I love you, no matter what. You know that, don't you?"

Anna nodded yes, and continued to the bathroom before Ella could see the tears forming in her eyes.

Two weeks had passed, and Anna was back to her old self. She had returned to work, to Dr. Montgomery's great satisfaction. At the end of the day at the drugstore, she had begun her walk home. Having walked a block she stopped to look in the window of the new dress shop. In the window were the long-flowing, skirted dresses, in different floral patterns, with full shoulder pads, like the defiant movie star Greta Garbo had worn in her latest movie. The sign in the window announced, "Just off the Paris Runway." Anna thought, how beautiful, I should go in and look. There are only two weeks until graduation. I deserve something new.

Just as she reached for the door, someone grabbed her arm hard from behind. She turned and was face to face with Vic.

"What do you want, Vic?" Anna asked.

"Well, I haven't seen you for a while, and I have been missing you," he answered.

"Vic, there is nothing that you and I have to talk about. What's done is done; what we had is over. Let me go!" Anna said, wrenching her arm away from Vic.

"Have you forgotten what I told you? You belong to me! And nothing is over until I say it's over! And tell that sister of yours that I intend to see my son!" Vic sneered.

Vic's words stung as if he had slapped her. "His son!" Aileen had never said who had raped her. Quinn's green eyes. Suddenly it all came together.

"Go to hell, Vic!" She said, turning to walk away. Vic lifted his hand to slap her.

Someone grabbed Vic's arm from behind and spun him around, hitting him and knocking him to the concrete sidewalk. Vic crawled to the building wall. He sat against the wall underneath the big display window, while using his hand to wipe the blood from his lip.

Vic looked up to see both Carlton and Hugh, not knowing which one hit him and noticing that they were both equal his size. He said. "Hey look, we were just talking."

Carlton replied, "Well I think this conversation is over; don't you think so?"

Scrambling to get to his feet and then walking away to his car. Vic replied, "Yea man, I guess it is, for now."

"What are you guys doing here?" Anna asked, "Are you shopping for new dresses? That polka dot one would fit you nicely, Hugh?"

They all laughed, "Nope, just thought you might want a ride home, that's all."

Walking home from work the next evening, Anna spotted Beth perched on a bench on the screened-in porch. She thought to herself, Beth must be nurturing a juicy morsel of gossip today. Anna was reminded of one of Amy's pranks. Amy would stand near Beth's bedroom window, just out of eye range. Then she would talk as if she were whispering to someone about events and people in the Grove that never happened. Anna could visualize Beth's leaning further and further to the side of the bed until her large bottom almost toppled out of bed. Anna laughed at the thought.

"Hey, Anna! Anna is that you child? Did you hear what happened in town? They say that Vic boy almost killed that little Chinese wife of his. Almost beat her to death. Had you heard anything about that? Huh?"

"No, Cousin Beth, I haven't heard anything about that."

"The police got him in jail, though he'll probably be out by tomorrow."

"Sure is a shame that little girl here all by herself. And she lost her baby, too. Sure is a shame." Beth continued, murmuring to herself. Not noticing that Anna had continued walking.

Anna opened the bedroom door to find Amy at her desk looking over the brochure from University.

"Do you think dad will let us use the Studebaker to go into town?" Anna asked.

"Probably not, unless you have a really good reason," Amy responded.

"What if we said we were going to the movie; Wizard of Oz is showing. Everybody knows about that movie. We could say it's the last night that it will be showing. That way, he will believe us if we plead with him," Anna suggested.

"Okay, it's worth a try, but where are you really going?" Amy asked.

"I'll tell when we get there; you'll just have to trust me. By the way, how much cash do you have?" Anna asked.

"About ten dollars," Amy replied.

"Good, bring it."

Anna drove down the black tar road to Hwy 47 and headed into town. She pulled to a stop in front of Vic's café.

"I thought you were finished with this mess!" Amy fumed.

"Just get out Amy, please." Anna pled.

The two walked into the dimly lit, seemingly empty café. Sitting at a table in the very back was a small badly bruised creature. The right side of her face was double its normal size. Her tiny hands showed signs of trying fruitlessly to protect herself. Her eyes, staring were filled with fear.

"I don't know if you remember me" Anna said," but we met here a while back. Vic told you that I was one of your best customers."

Ah Lam nodded her head.

"What Vic did not tell you, however, was that he and I had been having an affair since before you arrived in town." Anna continued.

Ah Lam, painfully speaking through cut and bruised lips said, "I know who you are, Anna. Vic told me. He likes to brag to me about you and the baby you are having."

"I am so sorry," Anna said. "Vic is a violent man. I'm afraid that if you stay here, he will kill you."

"He said he hated me; he said he would kill me. I was so afraid. He choked me and said he didn't want me or the baby. But what can I do?" Ah Lam said through tears cascading down her swollen red cheeks.

"Is there some place that you can go before he gets out of jail? Is there some place safe? It needs to be some place where Vic will not know to look for you," added Amy.

"I have a friend in Langston City, Michigan. She has been in America for ten years. Vic does not know her or where she is. But I have no money. Vic gives me no money."

"If we can buy a bus ticket, will you leave tonight?" Anna asked.

"Yes, but where will you get the money?"

"Don't worry about that; just get packed, as quickly as you can."

Ah Lam went upstairs to the apartment she and Vic shared above the café and returned minutes later carrying two bags.

Anna drove the three of them to the bus station. Amy went to buy the ticket while Anna sat with Ah Lam.

"I hope someday to be able to repay you," Ah Lam said.

"Please don't worry about it," Anna replied, "consider it a debt repaid."

The three women sat together until the bus arrival was announced.

Taking her seat near the window, Ah Lam stood to wave out of the open window. "Goodbye, my friends," she said, waving as the bus pulled away from the terminal.

The following day, Anna was in back of the drugstore taking inventory when she heard the door slam.

"Where is she?" Vic yelled. "Where the hell is she?"

Anna peeked through the service window to see Vic, obviously drunk; his eyes glazed and wild like those of a rabid dog.

“Hey you” he said, wobbling toward the service window, “come here, you bitch! You helped her leave me. You have the nerve to help her leave. I will kill you! You think you are smart enough to make decisions for me!”

Hearing the raucous noise, Dr. Montgomery opened the door of his office.

“Sir, can I help you?” he asked.

“This has nothing to do with you. I am here to talk to that bitch and her sister. They think they are better than everybody in town,” Vic slurred.

“I’m sorry sir, but unless you are here for business purposes, you will have to leave my establishment.” said Dr. Montgomery.

At that, Vic took a swing at Dr. Montgomery, missing and falling to the floor.

“Call Sheriff Crane,” Dr. Montgomery said, taking the drunken Vic by his plaid-shirted arms, dragging him to the door and planting him on the sidewalk just outside the door.

Chapter 22

Aileen hadn't thought her letter showed any indication of distress, only that she missed him terribly and that Quinn asked of him every day. However, she had not been able to control her excitement at seeing his long athletic legs step from the passenger side of the dark blue, four-door Chevrolet and onto the graveled drive way. In his brown Windsor double-breasted suit and two tone brown and white shoes, Aileen thought he had never been more handsome.

She had been sitting on the porch, watching the two brown head youngsters argue over whose turn it was to push the swing and whose turn it was to sit. Aileen recalled, years ago, similar arguments she had had with David, the instant that their father had finished constructing the swing.

Corbin, as usual, made the engineering feat seem simple. He had cut a four-by-six piece of wood as the seat. He suspended the seat between two heavy links of chain, slung over the limb of the old, knotted oak in the front yard. Aileen, however, had thought it was genius.

So engrossed was she in the argument, that the unfamiliar car was halfway up the road when she noticed it. Quinn and Lilla had stopped to see who the unannounced visitors were as well.

"Daddy!" yelled Quinn, running to the opened car door.

"Daddy!" yelled Lilla, following in Quinn's tracks to the open car door.

"This is an explanation that will have to wait," Aileen thought, getting up from the rocker and running toward the car and leaping into Michael's arms. Michael caught her and swung her around in the air, kissing her at the same time.

"Hey, Aileen. Hey there, Quinn, you do remember Aunt Carol, don't you?" Carol said, exiting the driver's side door.

"Hope you don't mind that I went to the train station to pick him up. He wanted so much to surprise you two," said Carol.

Michael released Aileen and picked up Quinn.

"Lilla, this is Uncle Michael, Quinn's father." Aileen said, attempting a quick explanation.

Lilla looked as if she were trying to put the words father and daddy together, and wonder why it was that Quinn had both and she had neither. "Daddy," she said.

Michael looked down at the beautiful wandering brown eyes and scooped her up as well.

"Come inside," Aileen said, pulling open the screen door, "Momma is inside. Momma, look who is here!"

Ella appeared from the kitchen, wiping her flour-covered hands onto her apron. "Well, Michael, why didn't you tell us you were coming? My God, it is so good to see you. Aileen did you know he was coming?"

"Nope, didn't have any idea," Aileen said, glowing.

Michael bent to dislodge his two bundles and walked over to hug and kiss Ella on the cheek.

"Sit down," Ella directed, "how was your trip?" "Sorry for the mess," she continued, trying unsuccessfully to put back a stray red curl that had fallen into her face. "We're getting ready for the twins' graduation party this weekend. You are just in time. Carol, you and your parents are coming, right?"

"Yes, ma'am, Miss Ella, Mama and I will be here for sure, but you know daddy, he may be working." Carol answered.

"Michael, son it is so good to see you. Whatever you have been doing up there in Colorado has been good for you. Have you seen that dam, Hoover dam; that's all we hear about on the radio? It's supposed to be something grand."

"Yes, ma'am, Miss Ella, the Hoover Dam is something to see. It goes as far as the eye can see. As a matter of fact, I have crossed it a couple of times."

"Well, I guess I need to be getting home," Carol said, "Michael, do you need help getting your bag?"

"I'll help Daddy," Quinn offered, following Michael out to the car.

"I'll help Daddy," mimed Lilla headed to the car behind Quinn, before being scooped up by Aileen at the front door.

At the dinner table that night, the house was alive with conversation about Michael's many travels.

"How big is that dam, the Hoover Dam?" asked Carlton. "I heard it's as tall as Mount Everest."

"That's a bit of an exaggeration," injected Hugh. "Hoover Dam is just over 720 feet and Mount Everest is over 29,000 feet."

"Who cares, they're both tall and gigantic, and I can't wait to see them both," proclaimed Carlton between bites of roast beef.

"You know, Michael, as soon as I graduate, I am going to the army, so that I can travel all over the world like you." Carlton continued.

"Traveling can be great, but it takes you away from the people you love a lot. You have to really be sure that it's what you want to do," Michael replied.

"What's Spain like?" asked Ella. "The pictures I've seen make it look like a very beautiful place."

Quinn answered, "Spain has lots of people with big hats and donkeys!"

"How do you remember that Quinn? You were only three years old when you were in Spain?" said Lorraine.

"He has the memory of an elephant," replied Aileen.

The comparison of Quinn to an elephant set Lilla off in laughter, resulting in a table filled with people folding over in uncontrolled laughter.

"Did you want to drive over to your parents' tonight?" Anna asked after dinner, sitting on the porch.

"Not tonight, I think I'll just rest tonight and go over tomorrow," Michael replied.

"Okay, then I need to get Quinn and Lilla ready for bed. I'll see if I can get Anna and Amy to allow them to sleep in their room tonight. They shouldn't mind, since they just moved into their new room," Aileen said, walking toward the front door and calling for Quinn and Lilla.

With drinking glasses pressed firmly against their bedroom wall, Anna and Amy snickered.

“Quiet,” Amy chastened Anna. “They’ll hear you.”

The bumping of the iron headboard against the wood wall in the adjourning room made it evident that the two lovers were showing how much they missed each other, and that they still loved each other and appreciated being back together, body to body and soul to soul.

The smell of coffee brought almost everyone to the breakfast table. Aileen was still in bed when Michael joined the family at the breakfast table.

“What can I get you for breakfast?” asked Ella. “Is there anything special that you might want? We have bacon, scrambled eggs, biscuits, syrup and sausages. But if there is something special you would like, either I or one of the girls would be glad to make it for you.”

Anna and Amy looked at each other and tried desperately not to grin at the pajama-and-robe clad, handsome young man who had joined them, obviously tired after a full night of bed bumping.

“Just a cup of coffee for now,” Miss Ella, he answered.

“After last night, I’ll bet he needs that coffee,” Amy whispered to Anna, moving over so that Michael could take the chair between them.

“Get any sleep last night,” Amy snickered, causing Michael’s face to turn an immediate shade of red.

“Okay, you two leave Michael alone and get out of here before you miss your bus,” Ella said, with mock scolding.

After breakfast, Michael dressed and walked out to the car shed, where Corbin was working under the hood of the Baker family's car. Michael walked over to the side of the car, opposite of where Corbin was working.

"Nice automobile these Fords are, been thinking of getting one for Aileen and Quinn when we get back to Colorado."

"Yes, it has a great motor, can't seem to find out why this family is having so much trouble with this one. This is the second time in a month that they have brought this one in to me. I'm beginning to think that the trouble has more to do with the driver than the automobile," Corbin replied.

Michael moved over and sat on the tall metal stool near the workbench.

"Mr. Sumpner, I never had a chance to ask you properly for Aileen's hand in marriage. I had always planned to, but things just got out of hand, and we ended up making decisions without planning. I hope you know that I've always loved Aileen, and I meant no disrespect to you or Miss Ella. I hope you know that I will always do the very best I can to take care of her and Quinn."

"Um," said Corbin.

"I hope you know that they are my life and that I will never ever do anything to harm them."

"Um," said Corbin.

"I just needed you to know that, Sir. And I know it's late, but I'm asking now for your blessing over our marriage, Sir, if you would."

"Hum," said Corbin.

Looking at the ground, Michael got up from the stool and started walking toward the house, his shoes making crunching sounds with each step he made on the gravel driveway.

"Michael," Corbin said, "You've done a good job, Son. I am proud to have you as part of this family."

"Come here, I want to show you something," Corbin said. Walking to the far side of the shed, he lifted a gray tarp. "This was going to be Aileen's graduation present," pointing to the blue two door 1928 truck. "The boys helped me to restore it. I figured she would use it to go to University. She has never seen it. So I was a bit disappointed that I never got to give it to her. But I'd say now, that you have made up for that disappointment. She loves you; the two of you have a beautiful, healthy child, and you are doing very well in your business. As long as she is happy, so am I."

Walking back toward the house Michael turned and said, "Hey Mr. Sumpner, what happens to the truck now?"

Corbin smiled and said," Man, I have a house full of women. It passes down to the next one."

Chapter 23

Driving up to the circular driveway, Michael was surprised at how nothing seemed to have changed. He parked on the paved driveway alongside the blue two story, colonial-style house, with its white shuttered windows and long covered porch. The two formerly-white dormers had been trimmed in blue, but the rest of the house looked the same.

His mother's rose bushes lined either side of the sidewalk, which stretched the entire length of the yard, from the porch steps to the street. The apple tree on the right side of the house did not appear to have changed. The big oak tree next to Carol's bedroom window was still there. He remembered the many nights Carol had shimmied the giant limbs of that tree to escape her many groundings, and then used it to return undetected by their parents.

At the front door, Jennifer cried with excitement, "Aileen, Michael," while opening the screen door. She then grabbed Michael in a bear hug. "Oh Son, I have missed you so! How have you been? You look well. Let me look at you."

Releasing Michael, Jennifer looks down to see Quinn. "Quinn, how are you, Handsome?" she said.

"I'm doing quite well," replied Quinn. "How are you, Grandmother Jennifer?"

"Come in! Come in! Have a seat," Jennifer said, directing them to the cream-colored, chenille, camelback sofa in the formal living room, which was filled with French provincial furniture.

"Carol told me that you were here. She said she picked you up from the train station, I wish she had let me know, so that I could have come with her. We were so worried for so long. We didn't know what had happened. Never mind that now."

Jennifer, wearing a pink striped blouse with a collar that played with the ends of her new bob-cut blond hair, she was five feet tall at most and around 100lbs. Giving her the appearance of a humming bird, as she nervously flirted around from place to place. "Are you hungry, do you want something to eat? What about you, Aileen, are you hungry?"

"No Mom, we are fine, maybe later. Where is Carol?" Michael asked.

"She ran off to the store; she should be back shortly. Oh, Aileen has told me about your business and all the traveling you have been doing," Jennifer said, moving to sit in one of the large blue cushioned chairs in front of the sofa.

"Yes, Mom, my plan was altered a bit, but I am in the horse breeding and training business, which is what I always wanted to do, only Colorado, instead of Wyoming," Michael said smiling.

"Well did you ever get to Wyoming to see your grandfather's land? You know that land had been in the Crenshaw family for over a hundred years when your grandfather lost it," Jennifer said, pulling at a stray thread at the hem of her pink Capri pant leg.

"Yes, Mom, as a matter of fact, Aileen and I were able to purchase the majority of the property back. Some owners, however, were not willing to sell the property."

"Well your dad is in his study; you might want to go in and speak to him before dinner. Dinner is almost ready. I was just finishing the salad, nothing special."

"Your room is still the same. Do you want to take Quinn to see your room? I haven't moved a thing since you have been gone. Aileen, do you want to help me in the kitchen, while Michael shows Quinn his football trophies."

Quinn followed Michael down the long hallway to the closed door of his father's study. Michael tapped on the door.

"Come in," Peter Crenshaw said.

Michael opened the door to find Peter Crenshaw lying on a brown leather sofa, positioned underneath an open window. The wind was blowing the brown gingham curtains hanging on either side of the window.

Grunting, Peter got up from the sofa and met Michael mid-way the green Oriental rug which covered the entire floor. He gave his son a big hug and shook his hand.

"Good to see you Son," Peter said

"It's good to see you, Dad."

"And this young man must be Quinn."

"Hello Quinn, I've heard a lot about you from your Grandmother Jennifer and Aunt Carol," Peter said.

"Hello, Grandfather," Quinn replied, looking from one man to the other and noticing how similar his father and grandfather looked. Michael, a few inches taller, yet both men had thick dark brown hair and blue eyes.

Aileen peeked in the door and said, "Michael, Carol is here. Your mom said it's time to eat."

At the dinner table, Peter Crenshaw asked blessing for the food, as he had done at every meal for as far back as Michael could remember.

"Tell us about all your travels, Michael," Jennifer asked. "Let's see, Aileen said you were in London and Spain and where else?"

"Well," Michael replied, "I don't really get to see much of the cities that I travel to. When I get there I am mostly focused on the business at hand. I spend a lot of time in hotels, at horse shows, or at the ranches of my clients."

"Michael said he has been to Wyoming to look at the family property. He and Aileen have been able to buy some of it back, the majority of it," Carol added.

"That's great," Peter said, focusing on the water glass half-filled with bourbon, which he was holding in his hand. Michael glanced over and wondered how many glasses he had already had.

"It just sounds so exciting to me," replied Jennifer, "Don't you think so Peter?"

"Well, I guess it's as good a job as any, if you don't have a college education," replied Peter.

"Dad, you know I never planned to go to college. That was your plan, not mine."

Exploring the displays on the French provincial dining room credenza, Quinn asked, "What is this?" pointing at the beautiful crystal bowl with Princeton class of 1876 etched into the side.

"That belonged to my father," Jennifer answered walking over to pick up the beautiful sparkling crystal bowl. "He was your great-grandfather. Both of your great-grandfathers were Princeton men."

"A lot of good that did," Peter retorted.

Jennifer could tell that the conversation was turning into an all too familiar area and attempted to change the tone. "Quinn should be going to school soon; have you made any decisions about where he will be going."

"No Mom, we'll probably make that decision once we get back to Colorado," Michael answered." There are lots of very good public and private schools to choose from in Colorado Springs."

"Well, let's just hope he finishes high school and goes on to a good college." Peter jabbed.

"What do you mean by that, Dad?" Michael asked.

"I'm just saying it's better to have something to fall back on. Or he could end up like your grandfather, running all over the place and wasting his whole life and all the family's money on one pipe dream after another." By now, both Michael and Peter were yelling.

"Get your purse, Aileen, we need to go," Michael said, reaching for Quinn's hand and heading for the front door.

"Michael, please don't go. I was hoping you would spend the night. I had prepared beds for you." Jennifer pled.

"I knew it would be a waste of time," Michael said, once they were in the car and headed back to the Sumpners. "That man is as stubborn as a mule. One way or another, he finds a way of blaming grandpa for what happened with the land. He is just an angry and disappointed man, who never achieved anything and never had a real dream. All he ever wanted to do was to become management in some plant."

"But Michael, you said your dad had been a plant manager," Aileen replied.

“Yes, when we moved here, the company sent him down as plant manager. This was a promotion for him and the job he had always wanted. A couple of years after we moved here, the economy got worse. The plant closed, and he lost that job.

The only job he could get was at the saw mill, at a substantial reduction in pay. He always felt that if he had completed his college education, instead of marrying my mother, that he would have had more opportunities. So he goes around blaming everybody: me, grandpa and my mother.

After two weeks of continued prodding from Aileen, Michael agreed to a lunch visit with Jennifer. Morning dew had left the herringbone brick sidewalk slick, Michael noticed, as he rounded the corner of his parents’ house.

Jennifer was waiting in the backyard at the white, wrought iron table, seated in one of the four heavily ornate white chairs. The floppy straw hat shielded much of her face. She looked up to see Michael rounding the corner of the house near one of her garden of yellow and white gardenias. She stood to kiss him on his cheek.

“I’m so glad you decided to come by. I needed to talk with you before you left. There is so much about your father that you do not know. And now that you are a man and a father, perhaps it’s time you know, and maybe this might help you better understand him.”

“Dad has been the same all my life, Mom. He has tried to decide and plan out my life for as long as I can remember.”

“I know Dear, but you have to understand where you father came from in order to understand him now.”

“Mom, I have known this man all my life,” Michael replied.

“Yes, Michael, but you have not known him all of his life. Your father was born into a very prominent and wealthy family in Virginia.”

“He never told me that,” Michael said, pulling out one of the heavy iron chairs to sit.

“He doesn’t talk about it: he finds it too painful. His grandfather had made millions in the Tobacco industry. Your grandfather, Franklin, was his only child. Franklin attended the best private boarding schools all his life. He followed his father and the rest of his younger uncles and cousins to Princeton University. But even at Princeton, he was not a serious student. Princeton is where Franklin met my father and they became lifetime friends.” Jennifer continued.

The housekeeper, dressed in a chambray blue dress covered by a white bibbed apron, stepped down from the stone patio and placed a silver tray of iced tea and two glasses on the white iron table.

“Thank you, Mable,” Jennifer said.

“Princeton is also where Franklin met and married your grandmother. Your father was born a year after the three of them graduated. Just after your father was born, Franklin decided that he wanted to take a break and travel the world. He left your father and his mother in the care of your great-grandfather, while he explored the world.”

“Your father grew up having maids and nannies to answer to his every whim. The one thing he needed most and never had, was his father. When Peter’s grandfather died, Franklin inherited everything.”

Franklin had never bothered to learn about the operations of the business. He preferred to travel and attain worldly knowledge, as he phrased it. Coupled with a series of devastatingly bad investments and the crash on Wall Street the money was soon gone.

Michael watched as his mother filled the two glasses with iced tea. He noticed the graceful movement of her tiny hands. Hands of an aristocratic woman, he thought, who had followed a man with broken dreams.

"By the time your father was ready to follow the family pilgrimage to Princeton, the money was all gone. There wasn't enough money for him to go to college any place. The only property of any value left was the land in Wyoming. The land in Wyoming had been in the family for as long as anyone can remember."

The housekeeper returned, this time carrying another silver tray filled with sandwiches and condiments. She placed the tray next to the ice tea tray and returned up the patio and back inside.

"When Peter found out that your grandfather had sold that land in order to pay for one of his exhibitions to uncover tombs in Egypt, he was furious, and rightfully so. He has not been able to forgive Franklin since."

"Family friends offered to sponsor your father's education; he turned them all down. He chose to work while attending college, then he and I fell in love, we married, and he dropped out of school. He refused to take money from my family, he was too proud. He felt that he was man enough to take care of his own family. He would never be the kind of man that his father had been. So you see, Michael, he did have dreams, his dream was that you would finish high school and go to Princeton, as he never could."

"If he can't forgive grandfather after all these years, then how does he expect me to forgive him for trying to control my life?"

"Michael, your father is not well. He has not been well since the accident at the mill. Somehow he holds himself responsible. He is drinking more, and the doctor has warned him to stop."

Sipping from his glass of ice tea, Michael did not answer.

"Your father is not perfect, but no one is. He has his faults, yes, but he loves you and has only wanted the best for you. Please, promise me that you will talk to him before you leave for Colorado."

Chapter 24

After the graduation ceremony for the class of 1938, the Sumpner house was packed again with people, food, and laughter. Ella, as usual, had prepared a feast of all the children's favorite foods, plus a few new dishes she had learned about while listening to the new cooking shows on the radio.

The party had spilled onto the porch and the front yard. Corbin had hung kerosene-filled lanterns around the perimeter of the porch and in some of the trees.

The black police car coming down the tar-paved road with its silver lights on either side of the front windshield, looked like a loping beagle.

"Hey Corbin, can I talk to you a minute?" asked Sheriff Crane, stepping onto the gravel driveway.

"Sure, Sheriff," replied Corbin, handing Lilla over to Ella, while steering the Sheriff toward the back of the house.

"What's going on?" Corbin asked.

"Well, I hate to bother you when you are celebrating with your family, but we found Victor Beasley dead this morning."

"Victor Beasley, the guy who owned the café in town?" Corbin asked.

"Yeah, somebody beat the hell out of him, looks like with a bat. People in town said that your boys, Carlton and Hugh, had a fight with him a few days ago."

"My boys are good boys. They don't go around fighting for no reason, and they sure wouldn't kill anybody. Sheriff, you know my boys. You have known them all their lives," Corbin said.

"I know, I know," Sheriff Crane said, "But we have to check up on every lead, even the bad ones. Do you mind if I talk with the boys? Say tomorrow, could you bring them into the office tomorrow?"

"Sure thing Sheriff," Corbin replied, walking with the Sheriff back to the police car.

"What was that all about?" Ella asked.

"I'll tell you later, once everyone is gone," Corbin replied.

Sheriff Crane was sitting behind a gray metal desk, looking down at pictures scattered across his desk. "Sheriff, there is someone here to see you."

Looking over the top of his reading glasses perched on the tip of his nose, Sheriff Crane asked, "Who is it?"

"The Sumpners, Corbin and his boys," replied the deputy.

"Well show them in," said the sheriff.

Sheriff Crane, dressed in his uniform of grey slacks and grey long sleeved shirt, walked over to the door to shake Corbin's hand. The sheriff, a giant of a man measuring over six feet three and weighing over 250 pounds, moved swiftly for a man of his size. At just over fifty years old, his hair was completely gray except for a few streaks of brown. An athlete in his youth, he was also quite an academic, having graduated at the top of his high school class. He had spent over 20 years in the military before returning home to become sheriff.

Corbin spoke first, “These are my boys, Carlton and Hugh. Carlton is 16 and Hugh is 14. Boys, this is Sheriff Crane, and he has some questions for you.”

“Sit down please,” the sheriff said, pulling the chairs from under the window over closer to his desk.” Here, have a seat.”

Corbin and Hugh sat in the wood-back, cane-seat chairs.

Carlton, only three inches shorter in height than the sheriff, said, “I don’t want a seat. I want to know why you wanted us here.”

“Sit down, Son,” Corbin said to Carlton, “the sheriff is just doing his job.”

“Well, boys, have you heard about Victor Beasley being murdered?” asked the sheriff.

“What’s that got to do with us?” asked Carlton. “We hardly knew him, he was bum.”

“Yes, Son, but we have had a report that you and your brothers were seen fighting with Victor a few weeks ago.”

“There was no fight. He had his hand on my sister, and I hit him one time and knocked him down. He never got in one lick. And if he ever…..”

“Carlton!” Corbin interrupted, “that’s enough, Son.”

Carlton continued, “He was nothing, and if he had ever put his hand on one of my sisters again, I might have killed him.”

“Did you or your brother see him again after the fight?” asked Sheriff Crane, now sitting on the edge of his desk.

"No Sir, we never saw him again, just that one time," answer Hugh. "We didn't have any reason to see him again. He was not the kind of people we socialized with."

"Okay, well thank you Corbin, for bringing in your boys. Say Carlton, can you and your brother wait outside for a minute while I talk with your dad?" Sheriff Crane asked, opening the door and waiting for the boys to walk through, then closing it behind them.

"Corbin, you and Ella have done a great job of raising your children, your boys especially. But I want you to know just how serious this could be. We are following every lead that we get."

"Your son, Carlton, has quite a temper. If he doesn't get that under control, it may not be long before he is back in here again. I hope you understand that I mean no disrespect, but I deal with this every day. Does he have any plans for his life?"

Corbin responded, "He wants to go to the military."

Looking down at the papers on his desk, Sheriff Crane continues, "Says here that he is almost seventeen. That may not be a bad idea. Corbin, I' m not trying to tell you what to do but, as a 20-year military man, I can tell you there are a lot worst places that he could be."

"I have always wanted my children, especially my boys, to finish high school and get a college education," Corbin replied.

"Well, Corbin, now they have a program where a soldier can go to school for free, while in the military and still get paid."

"I don't want my sons killed in any war, like my brother. You remember what happened to John, killed in that damn war. Nineteen years old and dead in a useless war. And my best friend Robert, might as well be dead. He is still mentally trapped in that war. He never came home."

"I agree the war was hell. I served during the war, but there is little likelihood of another war for at least another fifty years. No country wants to go through that again."

Glancing down at pictures of Victor's beaten and bloody, lifeless body, scattered on top of a manila folder on the sheriff desk, Corbin said, "Thank you Sheriff, I will take your words under consideration." The two men shook hands and Corbin walked out the door.

In the back seat of the Studebaker on the ride home, Carlton continued his conversation, "If I had seen that Victor, I would have hurt him bad. He was lucky that I didn't do him like Dillinger."

Corbin, deep in thought, allowed Carlton to continue his rant until they reached the gravel-covered driveway.

"Enough Son!" he yelled, "Enough!"

Stunned, both Carlton and Hugh's mouths snapped shut.

Corbin, Carlton and Hugh went through the back door and into the kitchen.

"Are you hungry," Ella asked, vigorously wiping the spotlessly clean, red vinyl tablecloth. "We have already eaten, but there is chicken in the refrigerator."

"I am," said Hugh.

"Me too," Carlton said.

Ella opened the refrigerator and took out a platter of fried chicken, mustard, and mayonnaise. Moving over to the counter, she took a loaf of bread from the breadbox and began to make sandwiches. "There is iced tea in the refrigerator."

"So what happen?" Ella asked, once the four of them had sat at the dinner table.

"We'll talk about it later tonight," Corbin said.

"The sheriff thinks we had something to do with Victor's murder," answered Hugh.

"Yea, that sheriff is trying to tie us into what happened to Victor, but there is no way that I'm going to go to jail for something I did not do. Anyway, Victor got what he deserved, he was pure evil," said Carlton.

"Carlton, your mom does not need to hear this. Ella, we will discuss this later tonight," Corbin said.

In bed that night, Corbin turned to Ella, who was sitting in bed reading, with pillows behind her back propped against the headboard.

"Honey, there is something that I need to talk to you about."

Ella turned to look at Carlton. "What is it? Does it have something to do with today? Are the boys in trouble? You said that they had nothing to do with Victor. You said the sheriff said he was just following up on a lead."

"No, Baby, it's nothing to do with Victor. It's just changes that I have been noticing in Carlton. I am concerned about how he is changing, so fast."

"He's just growing up, Honey. All boys go through changes when they are growing up. I don't think there is anything to worry about."

"I know that, but the world is changing so fast; our community, the entire city has changed. So many different types of people are coming from all over the country looking for work and better life since the depression. I worry about the influence they are having on our children, especially Carlton."

Ella closed her book and placed it on the night stand. She moved closer to Corbin and laid her head on his shoulder. "We have reared our children to be good people."

"I know, Ella, but…I was talking to the sheriff today; you know he was in the military service for over 20 years. What I'm saying is that I think it may be best to let Carlton enlist in the army."

"Are you sure, Dear? If you are sure, then it's okay with me. It's all he has been talking about for the last five years."

"Ella, I was thinking of taking him in to see the recruiter tomorrow."

"Tomorrow!" Ella shot up in bed. "Tomorrow?"

"Ella, you just have to trust that I know what I'm doing, Dear. You just have to trust me."

At breakfast the next morning, Corbin said, "Listen everybody, your mom and I have to tell you something. After a long discussion last night, we have decided to allow Carlton to join the military."

"Wow," Hugh replied, "another year and a half, Carlton, and you will be gone."

"Well," Corbin said, "we actually decided to allow Carlton to join the military now, instead of after high school. We talked it over with Sheriff Crane, and it seems that there are programs which will allow Carlton to finish high school while in the military, and if he wants to, he can also get a college education for free while serving."

"Yes," Ella added, "it looks like a pretty good program."

"But what about war, Daddy? You said none of your boys would fight in any wars. If Carlton goes to the army won't he have to fight in a war?" Amy asked.

"Sheriff Crane and I were talking about that. He and I agree that there will never be another war like the last one. No country, not even Germany or Russia, would be foolish enough to put its people through an ordeal like that again."

"So this evening, when you get home from school, Carlton, you and I will go in town to talk with the recruiter about enlistment."

Later that evening, Carlton and Corbin headed to the car, "Wait daddy, calls out Anna, "I'm going, too."

"But you will be bored," Corbin protested, "We are not doing any shopping; we are going straight to the recruitment office and straight home."

"I know," replied, Anna," I have had time to think about it, and I have decided to enlist as well."

Ella grabbed for the chair behind her and slowly sat down. She had prepared herself for Carlton, but she was not prepared for Anna.

Two weeks later, the entire family crowded onto the train platform, waiting for Anna's train. Ella felt anxiously proud. Her little girl, dressed in a grey flare-skirted suit, beamed with excitement and anticipation. She would be reporting to Fort Carson in Colorado.

Corbin looked on as Ella made one last adjustment to Anna's skirt, her little feet in black, ankle-strapped pumps, eternally turned inward.

Carlton would be reporting to Ft. Sill in Lawton, Oklahoma for basic training. He would be leaving the following week.

Chapter 25

The pain came in the middle of the night, so severe that it caused her to sit straight up in bed and look down at her aching legs. There was no explanation for it, she had done nothing stressful. She had taken the prescribed pills whenever she felt the least bit of pain, and she was being careful to get plenty of rest.

"If I can make it to the bathroom without waking him, then Michael will not have to know." Aileen thought.

She turned her body to the side of the bed and attempted to step down onto the floor. The pain shot through her legs. It felt as if two opposing teams of mules were pulling the calf muscles in her legs. She fell to the floor. Michael jumped awake, looked over to Aileen's side of the bed, and then ran to the other side of the bed.

Kneeling down to face Aileen, he asked "What happened?

"I don't know," Aileen responded, "my legs, my legs they hurt so much."

She looked down at her legs, expecting to see some sign of spasm, but there was none. There was no redness; there was no bruising, no physical evidence of the severe pain she was feeling.

Aileen balled her hand into a fist and started to beat her legs. She remembered seeing the coach from the high school basketball team doing this, in an effort to break the spasm. Michael grabbed her fist and cradled her in his arms.

"We have got to find a doctor," he said. "We have to go home to Colorado and find the best doctor in the world."

"What will we tell Momma and Daddy? They cannot know, they must not know," she pled.

Michael nodded in agreement, "Okay," he said," they will not know."

He picked her up and laid her in bed and pulled the covers over her aching legs. He then went to the kitchen and brought back a glass of water and two pills, "Take these," he said "and try to get some sleep."

The breakfast table seemed a little quieter with Anna and Carlton missing. Yet the kitchen was still filled with the noise of a family busily preparing for the day ahead. Even though it was summer, there were chores to be done, and so everyone was up and at the breakfast table when Michael entered the kitchen.

"Morning," Michael said.

"Good morning, Dear," Ella replied. "Are you hungry yet? Where is Aileen? Is she coming to breakfast?"

"No, she wanted to sleep in; she didn't sleep well last night. I'll wake her a little later. I thought I would drive over to my parents this morning, while she sleeps," Michael replied.

Amy was busy reminding her parents of everything she would need for her trip to University, next week. She would be reporting early for training for her new job as assistant to the professor of music. She also wanted to get settled into her room at the boarding house next door to the University administration building.

For the entire fifteen minute drive to his parents, Michael thought of what he would say to his father. He would try to be as civil as he could for his mother's sake. As he approached the driveway, he could see his father sitting on the porch. He parked the car, and walked up the steps and sat in one of the painted, white wooden chairs.

"How you are feeling today Dad?" he asked.

"I'm doing pretty good today," he replied.

Looking over at the almost empty glass of bourbon on the small table next to Peter's chair, Michael said, "It's a little early for that, don't you think?"

"It's never too early for good bourbon," Peter replied. "Your mom's inside and Carol is gone to work."

"I didn't come to see Mom, I came over to talk with you. Mom is concerned about your health," Michael said.

"That woman worries about everything. I am doing as well as any man my age."

"Yes, but when is the last time you saw a doctor?"

"Doctor, for what; who needs a doctor? What do they know?"

"Dad, Mom told me what happened with Granddad. Why had you never told us the whole story?"

"What good does it do to bring up the past? It doesn't change anything. What does your mom know about my pain? Her family still has all their money. If she wanted to today, she could go back to her family's estate. Did she tell you that?"

"Dad, what Grandpa did was wrong, but he is dead now, and holding on to this anger is just hurting you. You can't see it, but mom can, and it affects all of us. You have a grandson of your own now. Isn't it time to let go of the past?"

“Um,” replied Peter “hadn’t thought about it like that, Son.”

“I just don’t want Quinn to grow up in all of this conflict and anger. He is a good kid, smart too, and maybe one day he will go to Princeton. But that will be his choice. Can we end this now, and start our own Crenshaw traditions?”

The screen door opened, “Michael, dear why didn’t you let me know you were here? I could have gotten Mabel to make you breakfast. Are you hungry; do you want something to drink?”

“No Mom, just came by to talk to dad. I was just leaving. Aileen wasn’t feeling too well this morning, so I need to get back. I’ll call you later to see how things are going.”

“Dad,” Michael turned to face Peter, “Please consider what we talked about today.”

Peter stood to hug his son, “I will, Son, I will.”

“And Mom, see that he gets in to see Dr. Kincaid soon.” He bent down to hug his mom, then gave her a kiss on the cheek. Jennifer, on the tips of her toes reached and pulled him back for an extended, yet tender, hug.

Michael opened the back door and walked into the kitchen. Ella and Amy were busily piling ice into a bowl and getting towels, running into the room he shared with Aileen.

“What’s going on?” Michael asked,

“It’s Aileen,” Amy yelled, “She is sick. She was throwing up all over the place.”

Grabbing the towel away from Amy, Michael ran into the bedroom. Aileen was bent over the side of the bed, trying to vomit into the bowl that Ella was holding.

"How long has she been like this?" Michael asked.

Maybe fifteen minutes after you left, I heard a crashing noise and came in to check. I found her on the floor, she couldn't get up. Amy and I put her back in the bed.

"Did anyone call the doctor?" Michael asked.

"Yes, he is on his way." answered Amy.

Michael rushed to the side of the bed and sat next to Aileen. "Baby, what can I do? Aileen, Aileen what can I do?"

Unable to answer him, Aileen lay back on the pillows and reached for Michael's hand. Michael leaned back against the headboard and pulled her head to his shoulder and held her close. He whispered, "I love you so. I love you. It's going to get better."

Ella and Amy took the wet towels and bowls out of the room. Michael continued to hold Aileen until the doctor arrived.

Standing in the hallway, after Dr. Kincaid had examined Aileen, Michael asked, "What's wrong with her, Dr. Kincaid? What's happening?

"Well, Michael her kidneys are not getting any better. And I guess that accounts for the pain in her legs, a lack of circulation to her extremities," Dr. Kincaid said.

"I have been in contact with some specialists in the Nevada and Colorado area. There is a clinic specializing in kidney disorders. According to their brochure, they are having positive results with some experimental drugs. As soon as we get back, I am taking her to their clinic."

"Michael, that would be a fine idea, if she weren't pregnant," Dr. Kincaid said.

"Pregnant?" Michael repeated, his face showing obvious signs of surprise.

"There is just no way, that she should be traveling; she is too weak. You run the risk of losing her or the baby or both."

Pregnant, Michael thought to himself, she never told me.

After Dr. Kincaid left, Michael returned to his wife. He climbed into the bed, lifted her head, and let it rest on his chest. "I love you so much" he said, speaking into her thick red hair.

"I didn't want you to worry," Aileen whispered, as if reading his thoughts and answering the unasked question.

"How many months," he asked.

"Four, as far as I can figure. Isn't it wonderful, Michael? A wonderful gift from God."

"Yes," Michael said, "a wonderful gift from God."

The sound of the creaking door caused them both to look up, "He wanted to see his mom," Ella said.

Quinn walked over to the side of the bed. "Mommy, how do you feel?" he asked.

Seeing the worry lines on his tiny face, Aileen replied. "I feel fine, Darling."

Aileen continued. “I feel so good that tomorrow your father and I are taking you and Lilla on a picnic by the pond.”

“Promise?” asked Quinn.

“I promise,” said Aileen, reaching over and pulling him closer. She hugged him and kissed him in the top of his head.

“Now go with Granny and let Aunt Amy get you ready for bed.”

As promised, the next morning, Ella helped Aileen to prepare a picnic lunch for Aileen, Michael and the kids. Michael carried the basket over the clover-cover hill and down to the pond. He spread the patchwork quilt on the ground under Aileen’s favorite tree.

Lilla and Quinn were busy chasing dandelions, which looked like floating balls of cotton being blown by the wind. “Quinn, Lilla come here, I have something to show you.” Aileen called.

The two brown-head cousins raced to see who could get to Aileen first. Michael bent down to catch the both of them before they collided into Aileen. “See here,” she said.

“Where?” asked Quinn.

“Right here,” Aileen said, pointing to crude carving on the old oak tree. “See the letters here. It says MC and AS.”

“What does that mean?” asked Quinn.

“Who put that there?” asked Lilla.

“Those are the initials your father carved when we were in eighth grade. Can you guess what they mean?”

Thinking for a minute, Quinn said, “It’s your initials right?”

“Yes,” replied, Aileen.

"Why?" asked Lilla

"It meant that your father and I would be together forever and ever." Aileen said.

"Why?" asked Lilla.

"Because Uncle Michael and I knew way back then, that we would be together forever, and we wanted these letters to be a symbol of that."

"Why?" asked Lilla.

Sensing where this conversation was destined, Michael asked. "Hey, are you two hungry yet?"

Sitting on the quilt next to Aileen, Michael took the fried drumsticks, bread, and napkins from the basket and served each child. "Hungry?" he turned and asked Aileen.

"Not yet; just let me enjoy the sound of the pond for a while." Michael gathered the two children, "Let's go on an adventure," he said, bending to talk to Lilla and Quinn.

"What kind of an adventure?" Lilla asked.

"A rock collecting adventure," said Michael, "let's see how many different colors and sizes of rocks we can find."

"Who wins?" asked Lilla.

Not realizing this would be a competition, Michael responded, "The one who finds the most unusual rock wins."

Aileen lay back against her favorite tree and remembered the first kiss she and Michael had shared standing at this very tree. How inexperienced, and yet excited, they both had been since it was the first kiss for them both.

Michael had promised that he would never love anyone else for the rest of his life. He would do whatever it took to make her happy, and he would protect her from any harm. She smiled, thinking that, at fourteen years old, Michael had their lives all planned out.

Michael and the children returned to find Aileen sleeping. The smile on her face indicated that she was dreaming.

“Quiet,” Michael shooed the children. “Go back and pick some flowers.”

“But I don’t want to,” Lilla whined.

“Don’t you want Aunt Aileen to have flowers when she wakes up?” Michael asked.

“Come on,” Quinn said to Lilla,” I’ll bet I can find prettier flowers than you can.”

“Bet you can’t,” Lilla cried, running toward the hill.

Michael lay at the opposite end of the quilt and watched Aileen as she slept. He thought to himself, there is just no way that I will ever lose you. There is no life without you. I promised you that I would take care of you, and I will. I will find the answer; there has got to be an answer out there somewhere.

Aileen stirred and opened her eyes to see Michael at the other end of the quilt.

“Where are the kids?” she asked.

“Another adventure,” Michael replied, moving to the other end of the quilt to sit next to Aileen. He planted a kiss on her lips. ”Remember our first kiss?” he asked.

Smiling, Aileen nodded. ”Neither of us knew what we were doing,” she replied.

"Best kiss of my life," Michael responded.

The brown hair flopping on top of the two heads was the first thing to appear over the hill. Michael begrudgingly said, "Guess they're back."

"Time to get back, I guess," replied Aileen.

"I need to go back to Colorado for a couple of days. There is a client coming in to look at two mares and I need to be there. I hate to leave you, but Miguel is not ready to do price negotiations. Do you think you will be okay until I return?" Michael asked as they made their way back to the house.

"Of course, I will. Mom and Amy and the girls will take good care of me. Just make sure you take care of yourself, and call me every day."

"Without a doubt," Michael responded, and stopped to kiss her softly on her lips.

Chapter 26

Excited by the prospect of leaving home and being on her own, Amy had denied the family the opportunity to go with her to the train station. She was, after all, an almost twenty-year old, college student living on her own.

Ella and Corbin had been allowed to drive her to the train station, park long enough to unload her luggage, give her a quick hug and kiss, and then they had been instructed to leave her at the platform. She could take care of everything after that.

After thirty minutes of nervous pacing, the familiar tweeeeeet of the train whistle sounded. Amy looked down the track to see the train pulling in. The door opened and the conductor dismounted first. Then she noticed a very well-dressed man step down onto the platform. The first thing she noticed was the shine of his black, wing-tipped shoes, the cuffed, black hound's-tooth slacks breaking just at his ankle, leading to his double-breasted matching jacket. She immediately recognized the face. "Dr. Montgomery," she sighed.

He seemed to look her way. She lifted her hand to wave, when a tall very attractive, dark haired woman walked into his arms.

Amy jerked her hand down and turned to the porter who was busy picking up and loading her luggage. Boarding the train, she noticed that there were not a lot of people aboard. Two young men in the brown leatherback seats across the aisle looked to be about her age. Maybe they are headed to University also, she thought.

She took a seat near the window so that she could enjoy the view as they traveled the fifty odd miles to University. Once off the train, she went to the office inside to arrange travel to her boarding house.

Mrs. La'Melle was standing on the steps of the white, two-story craftsman-style house, its shutters painted a light blue.

"Hello Dear," she said, walking to the fence and opening the gate to allow Amy and the cab driver through. "Just put them on the porch," she said to the driver, "one of the young men will get it for you."

Mrs. La'Melle a tall, busty, silver-haired woman of seventy, had once been a dancer in an earlier life, a story Amy would hear many times in the weeks to follow.

Unlike most of the boarding houses in the University town, Mrs. La'Melle's house was coed, a fact Amy had neglected to share with Ella and Corbin. However, that was of no consequence, since Mrs. La'Melle was a very serious house mother and did not allow any hanky-panky in her house.

"Come inside," Mrs. La'Melle said, strutting up the four wide, white steps leading to the white-planked porch. She opened the door and lead Amy into the parlor.

"Are you hungry, Dear? I'm sure we can find something for you to eat. We have already had lunch, and dinner is not for another two hours or so."

"No, I'm just a little tired and would like to wash up a bit," replied Amy.

"Let me get someone to show you to your room," said Mrs. La'Melle.

"Brenda, Brenda, can you come down and show Amy to her room?" she yelled upstairs. "And get one of the boys to take her things up."

Bouncing down the stairs was a blond-haired girl, wearing a green blouse and blue slacks with the pant legs rolled up to mid-calf. Amy thought she was about her same age. Brenda, Amy found out, was

Mrs. La'Melle's granddaughter, from Denver, who had received an academic scholarship to University and was living with her grandmother. There were four tenants currently staying in the house. Some tenants choose to share their room at a reduced rate, and some, like Amy, had private rooms.

"This is your room," Brenda said, opening the door and handing the key to Amy. Walking into the bright room with windows on three sides, Amy thought, I can be comfortable here. She sat on the side of the bed, which was covered with a pink and lilac floral bedspread with matching pillow cases. She gave the bed a bounce. I'm sure I can sleep on that, she thought. Dragging her luggage over to the corner, she sat at the desk which was in front of the window, facing the front of the house.

She turned back to Brenda, "Where is the bathroom?" she asked.

"Down the hall, there are two baths here, but one is reserved for Granny, and she does not share, so basically there is one bath."

"That won't be a problem," Amy said, "I have eight brothers and sisters; believe me I am accustomed to sharing."

"Well, I'll let you get finished unpacking. See you downstairs; dinner is at six on the dot." Brenda said.

At dinner that night, Amy was introduced to the two other tenants: Dr. Beckman, an elderly, semi-retired, widower who was a professor of English at the University. A small man with a dark beard except for a white triangular area in its middle, he reminded Amy of the artist, Toulouse Lautrec. Dr. Beckman only used his room during sessions when he had classes. A very thickly accented young man, Mahesh Chopra, was a mathematics student from India. Brenda and Amy rounded out the group of four.

The food, though not up to Ella Sumpner's standard, was tasty and filling. The conversation was lively and academic, Amy thought, not quite like being back in Clover Grove. These people had lived very active lives. They had traveled all over the world and seen many exciting things.

Nationwide, some schools had suffered the full impact of the depression. However, University had an enrollment of over 4,000 students and had just added three new buildings. The university was like a city all by itself. Clover Grove had a population of just over 2500 people. Initially, Amy was frightened by the prospect of finding her way around such a large campus.

After two weeks, Amy was getting to know her way around the campus. The music department was a fifteen-minute walk from the boarding house. Her other classes, once they started, would be in the building next to the administration building. She was beginning to see her decision to get to the campus before classes began as a good one.

Brenda had been a great help to Amy. Acting as guide, she had shown Amy around the campus and introduced her to the people she would need to know once classes started. Brenda, Amy found out, was part of a military family and had traveled extensively from one end of the world to the next. She had spent most summers throughout her life at University with her grandmother.

Each night after dinner, Brenda would entertain Amy with stories about the people on the campus. Like the other tenants, Dr. Beckman who, according to Brenda, had two wives to die mysteriously, leaving him with a substantial amount in insurance benefits. "Don't be fooled by the frugal way he lives; he has loads of money hidden away," Brenda said.

And Mahesh had been imprisoned in his home land and had escaped to America, where he had changed his name and taken on a new identity as a student, in order to get a visa. Amy listened but wondered how much of these stories was true and how much, was a product of Brenda's imagination.

One night after dinner, Amy was sitting across her bed, her head against the wall, reading over material she had been given by the admissions clerk. Brenda came bouncing into her room and sat on the end of her bed.

"Have you done it yet?" She asked.

"Done what?" Amy asked.

"You know, with a boy, slept with a boy." Brenda replied.

"No, I have not and I won't until I am married. Have you?"

"Of course, two years ago. You are probably the only girl on campus who hasn't." Amy gave Brenda a look of doubt and turned back to reading her pamphlet.

Brenda crawled over closer to Amy, "What are you reading?" she asked.

"Just this pamphlet, trying to make sure that everything is in order."

"Oh, that," Brenda replied. "Let me see." She reached for the pamphlet and at the same time pressed her lips against Amy's. Stunned, Amy at first wasn't sure of what had happened. She had heard whispers about certain boys in high school, but no one had ever said anything about girls. Amy didn't know what to think; she didn't know what to do.

"Get out of my room; get out of my room now!" Amy yelled.

Amy thought about telling Mrs. La'Melle and then decided against it. What if she doesn't believe her? After all, Brenda was her granddaughter. Amy thought, I don't want to have to find another room so close to the beginning of classes. She had been working with Mr. Eric Stanley, the assistant music professor, on vocals. He had said she had a natural talent; she just needed to work on her technical in order to get ready for competitions in the fall.

Days later, Amy was sitting on the piano bench at the old Steinway, waiting for Mr. Stanley, who was running late. She was playing chords and running vocals as she waited. The old Steinway had maintained its place on the stage of the auditorium for almost as long as the University had had a music department. She was reminded of the old standup piano at home. She began to sing some of the songs that she, her mom and sisters sang while doing the housecleaning.

From the back of the auditorium came the sound of clapping. She turned away from the piano and looked to the back of the auditorium. There stood the dashing Dr. Montgomery.

Walking toward the stage, he continued to clap his hands. "Continue," he said, "don't let me stop you."

"Dr. Montgomery, well, what are you doing here?" Amy asked.

Chapter 27

The smell of boiling fruit filled the entire house and usually signaled the approaching end of summer and beginning of a new school year. This week, Ella had been canning fruit and vegetables. The girls, Dana, Lorraine and Grace, with a sizable degree of reluctance, were busy picking okra, peas, corn, cabbage and tomatoes for canning. Hugh, when he wasn't at the school's lab, was picking peaches, pears and figs from the trees behind the house. Ella was proud of the crop from her garden, as well as from the fruit trees.

Aileen, who refused to stay in bed, had made her way to the kitchen table, taken a seat, and was preparing the meals for the day.

The vacant lot across the street had been the perfect place for Ella's vegetable garden. Corbin and the boys had plowed and cultivated the ground years ago. All that needed to be done at the beginning of spring each year was to turn over the new soil and mix in fertilizer before planting.

Lilla and Quinn enjoyed planting time, and now they were equally enthralled with harvesting, to the dismay of Lorraine, Grace and Dana, who felt they could get things done a lot quicker without their help.

The corn stalks towered over the garden like rows of silky head soldiers, standing at ease, arms swaying in the dry summer's wind. Lilla and Quinn had lost interest in their pea picking assignment and were now busy pulling ears of corn from the bottom of the stalks as high as they could reach, leaving a trail of silk and hulks behind them.

"You might as well follow them and pull the ears at the top. It's useless trying to get them to stop." Dana said, pointing toward the two-brown haired cousins.

That night at the dinner table, Hugh was eagerly discussing a test the school counselor had presented to him and a select few other students. Based on GPA and test scores, some students could skip some required classes and graduate a year, even two years, early. The counselor thought Hugh was a perfect candidate for the program and that it was a great opportunity for him to advance in his degree program.

Ella and Corbin assured Hugh that they would take a look at the materials he had handed them and would discuss the matter with him after the radio news broadcast.

Gathering in the parlor around the radio had become a nightly ritual at the Sumpners' home. Ella and Corbin would sit in their chairs on either side of the fireplace. Aileen would sit on the settee, and the younger kids would sit on the big crocheted rug of red, blue and green circles, in front of the fireplace. Together the family would listen to news reports of war brewing in Germany, Italy and Spain.

"Did you hear that?" Ella asked, "The Germans are moving their troops."

"Thank God, America never joined that League of Nations, or we might be pulled into this thing." Corbin replied. His decision to allow Carlton to enlist at such an early age was beginning to weigh on him. However, he found solace in the fact that America did not seem destined to join any of the wars.

"It's 1938, how can that Hitler get away with treating Jewish people like he is? I just don't understand it." Ella said.

"My teacher said that Adolf Hitler is a smart man, but that he is also very evil. He has opened concentration camps and is keeping the Jewish people there." added Lorraine.

"What is a concentration camp?" Grace asked.

"It's a place where you put Jewish people," explained Dana.

"Actually, the concentration camps are not only being used to imprison Jewish people. Political prisoners, people who marry outside of their race, as well as, those considered to be sexual deviants are also imprisoned there," added Hugh.

"Enough about that!" Corbin said.

"At least we know that Carlton and Anna are safe," Ella added.

Michael's last letter said that he had planned to be back at Clover Grove within the month but had to make a trip to Spain instead. Aileen's letter in reply explained that she missed him but was doing fine and understood the nature of his business. She begged that he be careful, considering the war stories being reported from Spain. She would be glad to see him as soon as he could make it back.

Each night at bedtime, Lorraine, now twelve, helped Aileen get Quinn and Lilla prepared for bed. Later, Aileen would lie between the two cousins while they read stories and then talked about life.

"Quinn you know how you said you wanted to be a big brother?" Aileen said, combing through his dark brown hair with her fingers.

"Yes," Quinn responded, continuing to look down at the open book in his hand.

"Well, you are going to be a big brother."

"When?" asked Quinn.

"In about two months," replied Aileen.

"Okay," Quinn replied.

"Are you happy?" asked Aileen.

"Sure, is it a little brother or a little sister?" Quinn asked

"We don't know yet; we won't know until it's born. Does it matter?" Aileen asked.

"I think I want a little brother. Little sisters are alright, but I don't need another one. I already have Lilla."

"Aunt Aileen can you read us another story?" implored Lilla.

"I can read a story," said Quinn.

"Sure you can," Aileen replied, "you are a great reader. And it's time for us to get you registered for school. It's time you started first grade."

"And what grade do I start, Aunt Aileen, what grade do I start?" Lilla asked.

The first week of September had brought rain. It had poured the entire day when the stranger, holding a medicine bag, knocked at the front door. Surprised that anyone would be visiting in this kind of weather, Ella opened the door.

"Come inside," Ella said, "my goodness, it's raining cats and dogs out there."

The man extended his hand to Ella, "Hello, I'm Dr. Carl Penske from the Penske Clinic in Rochester, New York. I am here at the request of Michael Crenshaw. He wanted me to see his wife, Aileen. Is she here?"

"Sure come on in. She is in her bedroom. Follow me." Ella said, leading the doctor down the hallway.

Ella knocked on the door gently. "Mama, is that you?" Aileen asked. "Come in."

Ella opened the door; Aileen was lying in the bed looking out the window. "Baby, this is Dr. Penske from New York. He said that Michael sent him."

Aileen turned to face the doctor, still standing in the doorway. "Come in, Dr. Penske." She said.

"Your husband went through a great deal of expense to get me here. I have a very busy schedule, so I hope you don't mind that I came in spite of the weather." Dr. Penske said.

"That's not a problem, Dr. Penske, I'm glad you were able to come."

"What is your area of specialty, Dr. Penske?" asked Ella.

"I am a nephrologist, but mostly I am involved in research."

"Neph, nephron, what is that?"

"Diseases of the kidney, Ma'am," Dr. Penske explained, looking over to Aileen. "We normally have patients come into our clinic, but because of the pregnancy we understand that it was impossible for you to travel."

Dr. Penske asked Aileen some routine medical questions and then physically examined her body. He asked for a urine sample, which he mixed with a solution in a small bottle. He put the cap on the bottle and returned it to his medical bag.

During the examination, Dr. Penske said that he met Michael a year ago while he and his family were on vacation in Spain. He was impressed with Michael's knowledge of the horse business. Michael had helped him acquire several quarter horses, horses that had done very well in races and brought in substantial purses.

"Who is your family doctor?" he asked. "Who will deliver the baby?"

"Our family doctor is Dr. Kincaid, and he will deliver the baby." Ella answered.

"How often do you see Dr. Kincaid?"

"He is here at least once a week," answered Aileen.

Two weeks after Dr. Penske's visit, he contacted Michael. The news was not good. Aileen was not suited for any of the medical trials being research at Penske clinic. There was nothing that Dr. Penske could do, the kidney was too damaged. The doctors at Penske Clinic would be willing to consult with Dr. Kincaid on how best to go forward with the baby's delivery.

There would be no miracle. Michael was devastated by the news yet determined to find an answer. He would not give up; there had to be an answer somewhere. He would contact the doctors at a facility in Germany. He had read about them in a medical journal. There had to be an answer. Aileen was an angel, she had never hurt anyone, she could not die. He would not allow her to die. It could not be. It was all he could think of, it consumed him. There is a cure, there is a solution, he thought, I just have to find it. I will find it.

His letters to Aileen had started to take on a quality of urgency. Aileen was concerned that he was traveling so much and to so many dangerous places, considering the wars going on all over the world.

Dearest Michael,

Please come home to me.

Dr. Kincaid has said that the baby will be coming within the next two weeks. He says the baby appears to be healthy. I can assure you that, judging from his kick, he has very strong legs.

Quinn has asked if he can name the baby. If it's a boy, he wants to name it Colt, for the first wooden horse you gave to him when he was four years old. If it's a girl, he has chosen the name Wren. He and his grandmother's favorite past time lately, has been watching the tiny birds playing in her flower garden.

I don't know how you feel about the names, but I have almost promised him.

I realize the news from Dr. Penske was not good. I can live with that, but I cannot live without you. You know, Dear, nothing will ever be able to separate us. We will always be together. I love you with all my heart, and there is nothing that can change that.

Please come to me soon, Darling.

Forever your wife,

Aileen

In the days to come, the nightly conversation between Quinn and Aileen would take on a more serious tone.

"Quinn, you know when we talked about Lilla's father, your Uncle David, and I told you that he was in heaven?" Aileen asked.

"Yes, I remember that you said he was looking over us all, especially Lilla."

"Yes, Dear, it's possible that in a few months you will start to hear people say words like die and dying. I don't want you to be afraid of these words. Each time you hear the word die or death, I want you to replace it with the word rebirth."

"Why?" asked Quinn.

"You know how you and grandmother planted seeds in her garden, and spring came and the seed grew into a tall and strong plant. Then when the plant was tall and strong and ready to be used, you and Granny picked the plant."

"I know."

"Well, sometimes birds will collect the seeds left by the plant. The birds will fly away and drop the seeds in some faraway places. The seeds will grow tall and strong just like the first plant. Well, that's called the rebirth of the plant."

"What does that mean Mom?"

"Sometimes angels take people to heaven, and it might seem that they are far away, but instead of thinking of them as dying, let's just say they have been reborn."

"Then Uncle David has been reborn, right Mommy?"

"Yes, Uncle David was reborn, so that he could look over us from heaven."

Each day Ella watched as her daughter grew weaker, knowing there was nothing she could do but pray. She prayed mornings, noon, and nights. Incessantly she prayed. "God, how do I wait for my child to die?" Ella prayed. "What is it that we have done to deserve this punishment? I have already lost one child; how can I part with another, so early in her life?"

Uncharacteristically, Corbin had become a fixture at the side of Aileen's bed, trying to keep her in good cheer with news from Anna, Amy and Carlton.

Michael arrived a week before Dr. Kincaid decided it was time for Aileen to go to hospital. Michael borrowed the 1928 truck that Corbin had rebuilt for Aileen, and drove her to the hospital. Corbin and Ella and the rest of the family followed in the Studebaker.

For two days, Aileen had slight pains, which came and went quickly. Dr. Kincaid was not too concerned. He had wanted Aileen in the hospital long before time for delivery.

The third day brought rain and the pain. The pain was coming quicker and more sharply. Dr. Kincaid said that it wouldn't be long now before delivery. Aileen was given gas to help with the pain. Michael sat at the side of her bed, anxiously holding on to her hand.

"Isn't it wonderful?" Aileen said to Michael, through the pain.

"Its wonderful Darling, it is so wonderful." Michael said, as he kissed her hand.

"Is there anything I can get you Baby?" Ella asked, standing at the other side of the bed, wiping Aileen's face with a wet cloth.

Corbin stood in a far corner, looking out of the window, as the rain pounded the empty spaces of the concrete parking lot.

The nurse popped in the door and said, “We are about to take her to delivery.”

Ella leaned over, placed her hand on Aileen’s cheek, and kissed her on her forehead. “We’ll be here when you get back,” she said.

Corbin moved to the side of the bed next to Ella, “See you when you get back, Baby,” he said.

Michael walked beside the bed, as two orderlies wheeled it into the hallway. He continued to walk beside the bed until it reached the door which said, “No Admittance”.

“You’ll have to wait here,” one of the orderlies said.

“I love you, and I will be right here when you get back.” Michael said, kissing Aileen softly on her lips.” I love you. I love you.”

“I love you.” Aileen said, her voice trailing as the orderlies wheeled her inside, and the door closed behind them.

Four hours later, Michael was still pacing the hallways and the waiting area. He found it impossible to sit still. Even when he tried to sit, his knees bounced involuntarily up and down, and he would be back on his feet again, pacing.

“Want some coffee?” Corbin asked Michael, “The girls can get it for you.”

Ella walked over to them. “The children have school tomorrow. We need to get them home, so that they can get some sleep.”

“Hugh can drive them,” Corbin responded.

“Are you sure Dear? He has only been driving a few months?”

“He can do it,” Corbin said.” I’m not going anywhere.”

Ella gathered the children and instructed them on how they were to behave once at home.

Corbin gave the keys to the Studebaker to Hugh and said, "I know you can drive them safely home, Son. Just be careful, it's raining pretty good out there."

Hugh assured his parents that he would be careful and he would call the hospital once they were safely home.

Finally, Dr. Kincaid appeared at the delivery room door. Michael met him halfway down the hall, trailed by Ella and Corbin.

"How is she? Is she alright? How is the baby? Are they alright?"

"They are both fine," Dr. Kincaid said. "You have a baby girl."

Taking off his white cap and looking down at it, Dr. Kincaid said, "Aileen did remarkably well."

"Can I see her, can I see her?" Michael said, reaching for the delivery room door.

"Not yet! Give the nurses time to clean her up. Go to her room and wait for her there." Dr. Kincaid answered.

Ella, smiling, placed one hand on each side of Corbin's face and kissed him squarely on his lips. "Thank you, God," she said. "A new granddaughter!"

The three of them rushed to Aileen's room to wait for her and to get a first look at the new arrival.

Forty-five minutes later Aileen was wheeled back into her room. Michael was surprised that she looked tired but not weak. Corbin peeked over Ella's shoulders to see how she looked. He, too, was surprised that she did not seem to have been weakened by the delivery.

"How are you, Baby?" Ella asked.

"I'm feeling better, Momma. Have you seen the baby? Michael, have you seen her?"

"Not yet," Michael answered.

"The nursery is closed, but they said they would bring her into my room for a few minutes," Aileen said. "I can't wait to see her. Where is Quinn? Didn't he wants to see her?"

Ella explained that the children had gone home to prepare for school the following day.

The nurse arrived minutes later, carrying the baby in a pink blanket, a tiny pink cap on her head. She placed the baby in Aileen's arms. Michael looked at the bundle in Aileen's arms and could hardly contain himself. Not wanting Aileen to see him cry, he turned to Ella and said, "She is beautiful, just like her mother."

Ella lifted the tiny pink cap and said, "Yes, she is. She looks just like her mom. Look at all that thick red hair. But Michael, she has your beautiful eyes."

The nurse returned to say she needed to take the baby and that the family would have to leave so that Aileen could get some sleep.

Michael said he was staying. He would sleep in the waiting room, in case Aileen needed him during the night. Ella and Corbin kissed Aileen good night. Corbin shook Michael's hand, and the two grandparents left for home.

For three days, Aileen and the baby stayed at the hospital. Dr. Kincaid said the baby was doing fine and could go home if there was someone there to care for it. Dr. Kincaid wanted to keep Aileen in the hospital for observation.

Michael said he would hire a nurse. Ella would not hear of it. She would care for her grandchild. Jennifer called to say that she would be able to provide whatever help was necessary. In the end, Ella took Wren Ella Crenshaw home, and Michael hired a part time nurse.

A week after the delivery, Aileen awoke and looked over at Michael sleeping in the chair next to her bed.

“Darling,” she said, “I want to go home.”

“Home,” he said, “to Colorado?”

“No, Clover Grove,” she said.

“We will,” he said, “but Dr. Kincaid said….”

“I want to go now,” she said.

“Okay,” Michael said, “Let me get the nurse.”

“No,” she said, “the nurse will try to stop us from leaving. Just help me get dressed.”

Michael went to the small metal closet attached to the wall, reached in and got the pink travel bag. He took out a yellow and blue flowered dress and helped Aileen into it. Taking her jacket from the hook in the closet, he wrapped it around her shoulders.

Slowing, he helped her make her way out of the hospital, outside and into the 1928 truck.

“Reminds me of our first trip to Oklahoma,” she said.

“Yeah, but this truck is in much better condition than the one we drove,” Michael replied.

“Are you okay?” Michael asked, pulling the truck out of the driveway headed to highway 47.

“I’m fine,” she replied.

At the point of highway 47 that turns to the Sumpner’s home, Aileen said, “Darling, can we go by the pond and my favorite tree?”

“Sure,” Michael said, “If that’s what you want.”

Michael pulled the truck as close as he could to the tree and parked. They sat and looked over at the pond for a minute. Aileen said, “Can we get out and walk down to the tree?”

Michael wanted to protest, but Aileen seemed so determined that he, instead, got out of the truck, went to the passenger side, opened the door and lifted her to the ground.

Carefully, Michael helped her to walk toward the tree. She seemed to be getting weaker, so Michael picked her up and carried her the rest of the way.

He leaned her against the tree. She turned to let her fingers trace the initial craved into the tree.

Michael ran back to the truck to get the tarp from behind the seat. Running back to where she was, he spread the tarp. “Here, sit here.” he said.

Aileen sat, leaning her back against the big oak tree. Michael put his arm around her and held her. Neither of them said anything for what seemed like forever.

Aileen grinned, “Best kiss ever,” she said.

“Best kiss ever,” Michael replied.

“I’ve always loved you, you know that, don’t you?” Aileen said.

“Always,” Michael said, kissing her long and tender.

They sat together watching the water in the pond and listening to the familiar sounds. Aileen laid her head on Michael’s chest and slept.

“We had better be getting home,” Michael said.

Aileen did not answer. Michael attempted to arouse her, but there was no use.

A wail came from beneath the tree, so loud, so primal that it shook the very roots of the old oak. Surely, the angels in heaven heard the cry. Surely, the vibrating sound had caused the gates of heaven to swing open. The sound came from the depth of the earth. Tears were streaming from Michael’s chin onto his chest and onto Aileen’s raven hair. He realized the wails were coming from him, from some place deep within his soul. He felt raw, exposed, helpless.

“Aileen, Aileen, Baby, wake up!” Michael cried.

“Aileen! Baby please wake up! I need you so! Please don’t leave me!” he cried. “Aileen!…. Aileen!…. God, Please!.... Please, God!”

Michael knew she was gone, but could not believe it. He sat holding her hands until it was dark and the moon was overhead. He gathered her in the tarp, gently wrapped her, and carried her back to the truck and drove her home.

Chapter 28

"I was passing in the hallway and was drawn in by that heavenly voice. I thought that God had released one of his angels to serenade us mortals today," charmed Dr. Montgomery.

"Please, Dr. Montgomery, there is no need to exaggerate," Amy said, blushing.

"Surely, you know that you have a voice that would cause angels envy. You have a very precious gift, young Ms. Sumpner," he said. "How would you like to get a soda over at the campus café?"

"Sure, but right now I have rehearsal. Can I meet you in an hour, say around seven this evening.

"Great, see you there," said Dr. Montgomery.

Amy found Dr. Montgomery sitting at a booth by the window at the café. His usual dashing, well-dressed and very handsome self, he stood when she approached the table. He helped her to remove her coat and sat across from her at the table.

"Would you like something to eat?" he asked.

"I did miss dinner tonight at the boarding house. So I think I would like a sandwich of some kind," Amy answered.

"Great, then I will have something also."

The waitress appeared wearing a uniform of blue, knee-length flare skirt, a crisp white blouse, with a red bow tied around the neck. "Welcome to the Wildcats Den," she said, "Can I help you?"

"Roast beef dinner special for us both," replied Dr. Montgomery.

"And what kind of drinks would you like?" the waitress asked.

"Cola for us both," replied Dr. Montgomery.

"How did you know what I liked?" Amy asked.

"I have ESP," Dr. Montgomery replied.

"ESP, what's that?" Amy asked.

"Extra Sensory Perception," Dr. Montgomery replied. "It's a new scientific theory that some people can know things, just by sensing them."

"But the truth is that I was noticing how long you looked at the roast beef picture on the menu. That's the total of my sensory perception-observation, plain and simple observation." Dr. Montgomery admitted.

They both laughed.

"What brings you to University?" Amy asked.

My friend, Professor Nichols, is a chemistry instructor here at the University. He sustained serious injuries in an automobile accident. I agreed to take on some of his classes here, while he recuperates.

"I'm sorry to hear that about your friend, and what about the drugstore?" Amy asked.

"I have been fortunate that business has been very good. I have taken on a new partner, as well as a new assistant. So this gives me a chance to dive back into teaching, which is my second love after pharmaceuticals."

"I didn't know you were an instructor."

"Yep, I taught for four years, while I worked to complete my doctorate."

The waitress returned holding a silver-colored tray above her head. She placed the plates and drinks on the table. "Is there anything else?" she asked.

"Just more napkins," replied Dr. Montgomery.

"And how long will you be lecturing this time?" Amy asked.

"I am not sure, depends on how long it takes for my friend to recover. I have taken a room in the faculty dorm. I stay on campus two nights a week, and then I take the train home for the remainder of the week." Dr. Montgomery said.

"So that means you are here every Monday and Tuesday."

"Yep, every Monday and Tuesday," he replied.

The conversation and laughter came easy to the both of them. Before long, it was as though they had known each other all their lives. Looking around at the empty booths, they realized that they were the last customers in the café.

Amy said, "Well, I guess we had better be going."

Dr. Montgomery motioned to the waitress, who came over and brought their check. He looked down at the check and handed several bills to the waitress. "Keep the change," he said.

Dr. Montgomery helped Amy to get her coat on, and the two walked out the door to the sidewalk.

“Thank you for dinner,” Amy said, as she began to walk away.

“Wait,” Dr. Montgomery said, “A gentleman always walks a lady home. By the way where is home?”

“I have a room at Mrs. La’Melle’s boarding house,” Amy replied.

“Aaah, the infamous, Mrs. La’Melle,” Dr. Montgomery replied.

“I see you have heard of her,” Amy said.

“Everyone who has spent any length of time at University has heard of Mrs. La’Melle. She is quite a character.”

Arriving at the boarding house, Dr. Montgomery opened the metal gate to allow Amy to enter. He stood outside the gate and waited until Amy was inside the doorway. She waved good night and he walked away.

For the next several weeks Amy would meet Dr. Montgomery at the café for dinner. They would share food and conversations about their daily activities, as well as, their future life plans.

Dr. Montgomery took her to an opera, plays, and to the local art museum. She was so impressed with his knowledge about art and artists like Monet, Renoir, and Leonardo De Vinci. He had even traveled to the Louvre in France.

One evening, she was at her desk writing a letter to Anna, when she was called to the telephone.

“There is a gentleman on the phone for you, Amy!” Mrs. La’Melle yelled from downstairs.

Grabbing her robe and tugging to get the sash tied, Amy almost tripped getting down the stairs. “Who is it?” She asked Mrs. La’Melle.

"I didn't ask," replied Mrs. La'Melle.

"But if he looks anything like he sounds, I would sure like to meet him." She said with a wink.

"Hello, this is Amy Sumpner."

"Hello there, Miss Sumpner, this is Dr. Montgomery, Stephen, Stephen Montgomery. Amy tried to shield the surprise in her voice. She had never heard him say his first name. She had never dared to ask what his first name was.

"I am back at University," he continued. "I was thinking, do you like jazz music?

"I haven't heard much of it, but what I've heard I can say I like."

"Well, there is a live band playing in Capital City tonight, how you would like to go with me?"

"I think I would like that, but I have classes early tomorrow."

"Don't worry, I promise to have you back home no later than 10:30, how does that sound?"

"That sounds great."

"I will pick you up at your boarding house around six this evening. I am borrowing my friend's car, so it should take us about thirty minutes to get to Capital City."

What do you wear to a jazz night club, Amy pondered, laying first one dress then another across her bed. She finally settled on an emerald green dress with a jewel neck collar and green pumps. Sitting at the dresser, she clamped her pearl earring onto each ear and pulled back her raven hair. She had never felt so grown up, not even at prom, when her dad had approvingly said that she was officially dressed to the nines.

She glanced at the clock next to her bed and realized that she had thirty minutes to wait. What should I do until he gets here, she thought, something I can do and not get myself wrinkled? She decided to sit and read over the jazz brochures she had gotten at the library. She had planned to read them earlier so that she could sound intelligent, if the subject turned to jazz. She took off her shoes and sat across her bed to read.

Bang, Bang, Bang! "There is a gentleman here to see you, Amy. Amy there is someone here to see you."

Amy hadn't realized how tired she was. She had fallen asleep with the brochures spread across her beautiful green dress. She jumped up, found her shoes, and ran to the stairs. Standing at the bottom of the stairs was the ever immaculately-dressed Dr. Montgomery.

The drive to Capital City was as predicted, about thirty minutes. It was still sunlight when they entered the door of a tiny building tucked between two larger brick buildings. Above the door, a hand-painted sign announced Arnold's Place; a single lightbulb on an electrical wire hung above it. The tight doorway made the entrance seem cave-like.

Except for the light on the stage and a few lights in the corners, the place was almost totally dark. Dr. Montgomery directed Amy to a table in front of the stage.

Dr. Montgomery took a match from the box lying on the small, round table, stuck it against the box, and lite the candle in the center of the table. "That's better," he said.

A waitress came over to their table. Dr. Montgomery asked, "How long before the band starts?"

“In about five minutes,” she replied.

“Good, I’ll have bourbon and a coke for the lady,” he said.

The waitress, a small very curvy young lady, wearing a tight, black skirt and white blouse, with a short apron gave them a snide look and walked over to the bar.

The band began to play. At first, Amy could not understand what was happening. The music seemed to come from everywhere: the walls, the floors, the doors. It made no sense to her. All the musicians seemed to be playing something different.

The waitress returned with their drinks and placed them on the table. Dr. Montgomery placed money on the table. The waitress looked at the bills. She then reached into the pocket of her apron for change. Dr. Montgomery waved his hands to indicate that she could keep the change, bringing a smile to the waitress’ face at receiving a considerable tip.

Dr. Montgomery took a sip of the caramel liquid in his glass and placed the glass back on the table.

“Can I taste your drink?” Amy asked.

“Have you ever had bourbon?” Dr. Montgomery asked.

“No, but I have had champagne and wine.”

“Then just a sip,” Dr. Montgomery chided.

Amy took a sip and frowned. She then took another and pretty soon, she found herself tapping her feet to the music, just as the other patrons were. Somewhere around the third or fourth sip, she had found the rhythm of the music.

As the car pulled up in front of La’Melle’s boarding house, Amy was more talkative than usual. “She had enjoyed the music. She had never experienced anything like it. It was the most fun she could remember ever having," she said.

Dr. Montgomery got out of the car, walked to the passengers' side, opened the door, and walked Amy cautiously up the steps.

"Are you alright to go inside, Miss Sumpner?" Dr. Montgomery asked.

"Yes, and thank you for such an exciting night," Amy replied.

"Then I'll leave you here. Good night Miss Sumpner," he said, kissing her on her cheek and walking down the steps and to the car to wait for her to go inside.

Of one thing Amy was sure, she was in love with Dr. Stephen Montgomery.

The telephone call came the next morning as Amy was dressing for classes.

"Amy, this is Hugh, you have to come home."

"Home why? Is something wrong with Mama, or Daddy are they alright?"

"It's Aileen, Aileen is gone. She died last night," Hugh said.

Aileen….dead, Aileen….dead, the words were reverberating in her head like a drum beat, but they made no sense; the two words did not belong together. It couldn't be, she was doing well, there must be something I can do, there must be time left to do something. All these thoughts and more crowded Amy's brain. And still she could make no sense of it. How? How? How could this be? Then….

"Is Mama okay? How is Daddy? Michael! How is Michael and Quinn?" She asked.

"They are all doing the best that they can, just come home as soon as you can, and Mama said for you to be careful."

Amy packed and took a cab to the train station. She did not know the train schedule. She did not care. All she knew for sure was that there would be a train soon and she would to be there to board it.

Amy boarded the train and took a seat near the window. Somehow the trip seemed shorter when there was scenery to look at. Unable to sit still, she thought she would walk to the diner car and get a cup of coffee.

Entering the dining car, she could see the tops of the heads of a couple. They were sitting across from each other at one of the booths. They were holding hands. Their matching gold wedding bands reflected on the heavily-lacquered table top. Whispers and laughter was coming from their table. Nearing the table, she recognized the man, Dr. Montgomery. She turned and attempted to walk away, but Dr. Montgomery glanced up and saw her.

"Miss Sumpner, Miss Sumpner, Please come join us." he said, standing to help her to the seat next to his wife.

"Darling, this is the young lady I was telling you about. This is Miss Sumpner. She is the student who has been helping me find some degree of civilized entertainment while at University."

Have a seat," he said, "my wife and I were just at University, visiting our friend Professor Nichols. He doing well and should be returning to work next week."

"My husband speaks very highly of you, Miss Sumpner. You're Anna's twin, right? Dr. Montgomery tells me that you are a very talented vocalist. He said you are poised for a dynamic career; pretty soon you will be replacing Caterina Baratto."

Amy looked first at Dr. Montgomery, then at his beautiful wife. She slumped down to the seat as though she was carrying a two hundred pound weight. Covering her face with her hands, she began to sob. Tears flooded her eyes, falling down her chin and onto the lacquered table.

"What's wrong, Dear? Do you need something? Can we get you anything?" Mrs. Montgomery asked, reaching into her purse for a handkerchief.

Amy realized that since hearing of Aileen's death, she has not been able to cry, and now, at the most inopportune time, she couldn't stop crying. Finally, she was able to mumble out the words of Aileen death.

The Montgomerys insisted that she sit with them. She declined and returned to her lone seat in the passenger compartment.

Chapter 29

The wooden double doors opened, and Michael began the longest walk of his life. Michael held on to Quinn's hand, as they began the journey toward the rose tinted metal casket in the front of the church. Michael could feel his feet move forward, but the casket was moving farther and farther away. With each step he took forward, it seemed the flower-covered rose box moved further away. He thought about the girl he fell in love with; so beautiful, so trusting, so full of life and so loving.

The pews on either side of the aisle were filled with faceless people. Unaware of their presence, Michael's only thoughts were of how Aileen had been stolen from him. He thought about all that they had accomplished and the plans they had to do so much more. He was stirred from his trance when Quinn released his hand and walked over to the casket to straighten the ribbon reading "Reborn".

Quinn had insisted that the white ribbon attached to the family spray of purple lilacs, pink lilies, white baby's breath, and lavender gladiolus would have the word "Reborn" in golden letters.

Michael, tear stained napkin in his hand, walked over, took Quinn's hand, and they returned to the first pew. Corbin sat next to Quinn, with his arm draped around Ella's shoulder. Anna and Carlton had arrived two days before the service and were seated on the second pew between the younger girls, Dana, Lorraine and Grace. Hugh and Amy sat at the other end of the second pew. The entire family was in attendance, except for Lilla and Wren, who were home with Michael's mom, Jennifer.

Ella's gaze was fixed on the rose-tinted casket. She thought of the funeral director's words. "It's a beautiful choice, the color is perfect."

At the time, she had been too weak to answer such an asinine statement. When is a casket ever perfect for someone you love? Who cares what color a casket is when it carries your heart, your child, your life? She had wanted to say these things, but what good would it have done to take out her vengeance on a funeral director, who was just doing his job.

Instead, she had stood next to Michael as he went through the list that Aileen had left. The casket, according to Aileen, was not to be expensive. It was not to be over decorative, simple, she wrote.

In the hope chest at the foot of her bed, Aileen had left a manila folder containing letters addressed to Michael, Quinn and Wren.

Letters to Michael, Quinn and Wren from Aileen

November 1, 1938

My dearest Michael,

How do I say goodbye to the man who has been my very life since I was fourteen years old. I don't even know where to start. Know that you are my heart. Know that there is nothing, not even death, that can separate us.

I know the kind of man you are, and I so appreciate the father that you have been for Quinn. I know that our children will be well taken care of, because you love them.

My love for you will never die. However, when the time comes and you find the right person, I hope that you will move forward with your life. What I'm saying to you, Darling, is that I fully understand that your life will not end when I'm gone. I want nothing less for you than happiness. So if you find someone to love, then love again, Michael. Promise me that you will love again.

I know that I don't need to say this, but be sure that the children know that their mother loved them with all her heart. Let them know that I would never have left them if it had been my choice. As you tuck them in bed each night, please give them a kiss and tell them it is from their mother.

I know that you will have to take the children back to Colorado, but promise me that you will allow my parents to be an active part of their lives. I am so proud of you for resolving the conflict between you and your father. And so, it is my hope that you will allow your parents to be active in the development of our children. It is so important that children know where they came from.

As time passes and memories fade, try to hold on to all our firsts. Take with you wherever you go, whatever you do, the knowledge that our love for each other was as close to perfect as any love could be.

I love you with all my heart.

Your wife,

Aileen

November 1, 1938

Precious Wren,

My little girl, Wren, I loved you long before I saw your face. And when I saw your face, I loved you even more. You have the gift of your father's beautiful blue eyes. You also have the gift of a father who loves and adores you.

If there is anything that I regret in all of my life, it is that I had such a short time to spend with you. Believe me, I have counted the time almost to the second. For two weeks, I was allowed to hold you twice per day, that's 14 times. I only had fourteen times to hold you close to my heart and listen to the sweet sounds you made.

Your dad will always do the best for you. He, like your grandfather Corbin, will work hard to provide for you and your brother Quinn. He will protect you from harm, as my dad did for me. You and Quinn are blessed to have such an incredible father. Your grandmother, Ella, also loves you, and so if there is ever something you need or that you need to talk about, give her an opportunity to help.

I love you with all my heart, and nothing can change that. Your father will kiss you each night before bed. If he ever forgets, remind him that he is to kiss you for me as well.

One day Quinn will explain to you that I am always near; he will explain to you where to look for me. Know, Darling, that I am always, always, near you. Do your best in school and try to find joy in life.

As I write this letter, I am looking at you in your hospital crib. Because I never know which will be our last visit, at the end of each visit, I will take you in my arms and I will kiss you from your feet to the top of your head, so that you are covered in my love. Darling, you are covered in my love today and always.

Your Mother,

My Darling Quinn

The best part of my life has been the six years that I have been your mom. You are my special little man. In our long talks, we have discussed what happens when I am no longer here to read with you each night. Remember that we decided that I would always be near the North Star. The North Star is always the brightest star and the easiest to see. One day, Wren will ask you how to find me, and you will have to tell her to look in the sky for the North Star, and I will be looking down at you both.

Remember our discussion on rebirth? I have been reborn so that now I am everywhere that you and dad and Wren are. I am looking over you always.

I love you so much, more than this piece of paper could possibly hold. I will never leave you or Wren; I will always be near you. Remember that every living thing has two parts; the mortal body and the soul. The mortal body will someday die, but the soul lives on forever. So remember that you and I are connected through our souls, and we will never, ever part from each other.

If I could have controlled my mortal body, I would never have left you. But that is not what God had planned. God knows best. He knew that my soul would be with you and Wren forever.

Always respect your father. He is a good man. He has been a good husband to me and a great father for you and Wren. He is hurting now, and he needs you to be there with him. One day, you will become a young man, and you may question some of the ways of your father. That is a natural part of growing up. You must remember, though, that your father loves you and will never do anything to hurt you. Anything he does will be because he loves you and your sister.

Do your best in school: learn all that you can. And be happy! Never hurt anyone unnecessarily. Be kind. Say your prayers both morning and night. Watch over your little sister. Mother loves you and always will.

Your Mother,

She had outlined her funeral program: The service was not to last more than one hour.

Processional

Hugh will read bible verses

Old Testament Lamentations 3:22-26

22Because of the Lord's great love we are not consumed, for his compassions never fail. 23 They are new every morning; great is your faithfulness. 24 I say to myself, "The Lord is my portion; therefore I will wait for him."25 The Lord is good to those whose hope is in him, to the one who seeks him; 26 it is good to wait quietly for the salvation of the Lord.

New Testament I Thessalonians 4:13-14

Brothers and sisters, we do not want you to be uninformed about those who sleep in death, so that you do not grieve like the rest of mankind, who have no hope. 14 For we believe that Jesus died and rose again, and so we believe that God will bring with Jesus those who have fallen asleep in him.

Song Amazing Grace Amy Sumpner

Poem Read by Carlton Sumpner Robert Frost

"They were welcome to their belief"

Grief may have thought it was grief. Care may have thought it was care.

They were welcome to their belief, the over important pair.

No, it took all the snows that clung to the low roof over his bed,

Beginning when he was young, to induce the one snow on his head.

But whenever the roof came white the head in the dark below

Was a shade less the color of night, a shade more the color of snow.

Grief may have thought it was grief. Care may have thought it was care.

But neither one was the thief, of his raven color of hair.

Reflection Anna Sumpner

Acknowledgement Michael Crenshaw

Though hurt was evidenced by the tears in his eyes, a hint of a smile curled at the corner of Corbin's lips, as he thought, so typical of Aileen, his hazel-eyed little girl. Never did anything the way anyone else would. She was so prepared to go that she had almost successfully prepared everyone she loved for her departure. True to her own belief system, even her funeral would be nontraditional.

At home that evening after the funeral, Ella and the girls were busy in the kitchen, setting out the food that had been prepared and delivered by the neighbors. The house again was filled with family, friends, and mixtures of aromas from baked ham, to fried chicken, to casseroles, to pies. Amy tried unsuccessfully to get Ella to go to her bedroom and rest. Ella would have none of it. She had a house full of guests, and she was going to see to it that they were treated properly.

Corbin had found a place of solitude in the back yard where he could sit in contemplation.

Michael, still in his black suit pants and dress shirt, sleeves rolled up to the elbow, was tossing a football with Quinn. Ella could see the two through the kitchen window.

Michael was tall, with an athletic body, dark hair and blue eyes. Quinn, it seemed would be shorter and was a bit awkward with sports, his green eyes watching intensely as he ran to catch the ball.

Ella thought back to David, her son. David was the only Sumpner child to have blue eyes and blond hair. Though Corbin knew, just as she now knew, they had discussed the issue of David's conception only once.

Corbin had loved David and had never treated him with any less compassion than he did any of the other children. This was evidently true of Michael and Quinn. The love they shared was undisputable.

So similar were the two men: loving fathers, gentle in nature, strong in conviction, dedicated and hardworking, protective of the ones they love. Ella thought to herself, "Did my daughter marry a man like her father, or did she create one?" Either by design or accident, Aileen had married a good man, Ella thought.

Acknowledgments

Thank you to all my friends and family members who encouraged me to write this book.

To my advisor, editor and husband, Kenneth, who read every page as I wrote them, though sometimes, begrudgedly. Thank you for keeping me on track. Thank you for having the courage to force me to justify my work. I will always appreciate you for that.

Thanks to my parents, Alvin and Connie Green, who taught me to see reading as an adventure, and to see writing, as a way of self-expression.

I thank God for the challenges of my life, challenges that, at the time, I did not understand. But without these challenges, I would not have had the wisdom to write this book.

Finally, thank you to my ancestors, upon whose lives this book is based.

Postscript

Thank you, classmate, lifetime friend, editor extraordinaire, and fellow Clover Grove resident, Loretta William Noiel for the exceptional detail work in the revision of this my first novel.

www.ingramcontent.com/pod-product-compliance
Lightning Source LLC
Chambersburg PA
CBHW030816310726
48980CB00006B/516/J
9781678156251